# THE DIARY OF
# A YOUNG LADY OF FASHION
# IN THE YEAR 1764-1765

# THE DIARY OF
# A YOUNG LADY OF FASHION
# IN THE YEAR 1764-1765

---

## BY MAGDALEN KING-HALL

---

MEREDITH PRESS · NEW YORK

# CONTENTS

# FOREWORD

I have been asked by my publishers to write a short fore-word to this new edition of the *Diary of a Young Lady of Fashion*.

I was nineteen when I wrote it as an escape from the boredom of living at a select seaside resort, the inhabitants of which seemed, to the impatient eyes of youth, to consist mainly of formidable old ladies being dragged along the 'front' in bath chairs by ancient men who looked as though they ought to be in bath chairs themselves.

I had been scribbling since childhood—writing was in the family—and my sister's encouragement, and her sug-gestion that I should write a novel in the form of an eighteenth-century diary nerved me to make a serious attempt at authorship. After some delving in the local public library, I plucked up my courage and wrote the opening sentences of the *Diary* on the back of an old envelope. I set the earlier scenes of the book in Northern Ireland. My mother's family came from those parts, and I had spent happy times there as a child. There was nothing autobiographical about my heroine Cleone Knox, who was lively and reckless, and surprised me, when I had finally got her safely married, by demanding a family of twelve children.

The book was refused by several publishers before it was accepted, and eventually published in November 1925.

I had taken shelter behind the pseudonym of 'Alexander Blacker Kerr', the supposed editor of the diary. All the same, it never occurred to me that the book would be presented and accepted as a genuine diary. I was disappointed that it came out with a plain jacket. Lord Darling, the eminent judge, gave it a long and enthusiastic review, and it rapidly became a best-seller in England and the U.S.A. This seemed to me like drawing a winning ticket in a sweepstake.

Inevitably some critics suspected the genuineness of the diary, and there were many speculations about its possible authorship, some more flattering than I deserved.

By now it was obvious that keeping up the secret would help 'Alexander Blacker Kerr's' literary career more than mine, and the fact that I had written the *Diary* was 're-leased' to the Press. What halcyon days the 'Roaring Twenties' must have been, one feels, seeing it all now as though through the wrong end of a telescope, when such a small mystery could hit the headlines!

I have been asked what my feelings are at seeing the *Diary of a Young Lady of Fashion* in print again forty years later. The answer is gratification (what author would not feel the same?) and the hope that the book may still give some moments of amusement and distraction to modern readers.

MAGDALEN KING-HALL
September 1966

# IRELAND

*March 3rd*

This morning had a vastly unpleasant interview with my Father. Last night, Mr. Ancaster, who is the indiscreetest young man alive, was seized suddenly while riding home along the shore with the desire to say good night to me. He climbed the wall, the postern gate being locked at that late hour, and had the Boldness to attempt to climb the ivy below my window; while but half way up the Poor Impudent young man fell. (If he hadn't Lord knows what would have happened for I am terribly catched by the Handsome Wretch.) As ill luck would have it Papa and Ned, who were conversing in the library, looked out at that moment and saw him lying Prostrate on the ground!

No need to describe the scene that followed. My father it seems thinks me guilty of Indiscretion and Immodesty, though why I don't know, for I was sound asleep the whole time and never heard so much as an Oath (and I dare swear there were plenty flying round!). My father said some mighty unkind things to me this morning and I wept loudly for more than Half an Hour.

Poor Mr. A. from all accounts is a Scoundrel, a Libertine and a Blackguard, and I have been forbidden ever to see, speak or indeed think of him again. Well, we shall see.

I own I cannot imagine how it will all end. Pray Heaven there will not be a Rencontre between either of my Indignant male relatives and my unlucky admirer. 'Twould make a Scandal in the county we should never hear the end of.

Men are such Damnable Fools there is no saying what they will do in a fury.

### March 4th

Kept to my room to avoid the sour glances that are cast at me if I venture below. My father as grim as death will not say a word to me. Ned puts on monstrously Virtous Prudish Airs. In short I am made to feel I am in disgrace. Declare I cannot see how I am to blame if a Foolish Headstrong young man attaches himself a trifle too warmly to me. Tried on my new striped silk gown which becomes me excessively well. Poor Mr. A. I doubt will never see me in it.

### March 5th

Rain outside and gloom inside the house. Am vexed with all and everything, the weather, my father, Ned, Mr. A.'s Imprudence and the striped silk which has split under the arms to my vast annoyance. My father and Ned out shooting Seals on the rocks. I hope Ned may come home Better humoured.

### March 6th

This morning Betsy, looking very sly, brought me a Note from Mr. A., vowing Eternal Devotion and breathing horrible Vengeance against my hard hearted parent and Ned.

It seems that Mr. A. has entirely spoilt his Crimson Plush Suit, which is all Muddied and Filthy from his lying on the damp ground. Why he was riding in his best suit he alone can explain. Did he expect I should be so foolish as to admit him at that hour of the night?

At all events he holds my poor Charms responsible for this damage, and vows that nothing but a kiss will compensate him!

My father came in while I was reading it, which made me very confused. Dropped it on the fire but he gave me a suspicious glance.

### *March 8th*

Am to leave to-morrow for Ballywiticock House, to stay with my Cousin Charlotte, so my father announced to me yesterday. See plainly enough that this is nothing but a plot to keep me from Mr. A. Urged the rain, and bad roads in vain. Swore I could not abide Coz. Charlotte's company for a day, far less a week. My father like all his Sex prides himself on his determination. I see Ned's doing in this. I could box his ears !

### *March 9th*

Off to Ballywiticock in a post chaise, with Betsy, my New Calash (vastly pretty), and 2 Fox Hounds to be delivered to Cousin Noll. Gave my father as stiff an embrace as a dutiful daughter well can on parting.

To my great amazement, we drove through Portaferry, though 'tis the longer Route. Suspect another of my Parent's Ruses in this. He feared I should see Mr. A. in passing Castle Ancaster.

To my mortification, I noticed Sly Smiles and Winks as we passed through the square. I dare swear Betsy has told the entire village of my Disgrace. 'Tis marvellous how quickly a piece of Scandal spreads in Ireland. Cannot comprehend how anyone can contrive to have a Lover in such a talkative country, yet I believe 'tis occasionally done !

A fine day and the countryside very pretty. Betsy and me had a serious talk about Mr. Ancaster. In her opinion my father will never admit the idea of a Match between one of that Family and me. He thinks them a Poor and Dissolute Race, but this is nothing to me, who Thank Heaven will have enough fortune when I am of age to support three husbands, and as for Dissoluteness—as far as I can observe 'tis a failing common to most men!

A most diverting little incident occurred at Newtown, where we stopped for refreshments. As I left the Chaise, a Military Officer, as proper a looking young man as you could hope to see, caught sight of me and followed me into the Inn. Had the boldness to seat himself opposite me at table, and watch me so closely as I drank my rum and milk that I nearly choked with embarrassment. After smiling coyly and casting "doux yeux" at me for several seconds, he touched my shoe softly under the table with his foot.

This made me blush! Had a violent desire to laugh, but contrived to compose my features into the expression of severe and outraged Modesty which I supposed a Virtous Young Female in my position ought to wear. Rose with Awful Dignity and went out into the yard, leaving the poor young man mortified. There I found a great to do. The Hounds profiting by my absence had escaped from Betsy's clutches, and after slaying three of the landlord's fowls had run down the Village street as fast as their legs could go! Not a soul had their Wits about them sufficiently to capture the Wicked Beasts.

At this moment the Military Gentleman emerged, and hearing of the Disaster set off instantly on horseback in their pursuit.

After a chase of more than Half an Hour, they were discovered in the Papist Churchyard, eating a morsel of meat stolen from a Flesher's. A cry of "sacrilege" was raised, and they were dragged back to the inn, the more Ardent Romans in the Throng pelting them with stones.

The Military Gentleman in a great Sweat and panting from his exertions, led the captive monsters in triumph to my feet. 'Twas only Civil to speak affably to him after such an excessive display of gallantry. If a young Man is Handsome enough one can forgive him anything!

In short he rode by my side for the rest of the journey, and we conversed very agreeably together. He was a very civil Genteel young man, but I thought it more prudent to bid him Adieu before reaching Ballywiticock.

Coz. Charlotte received me with her customary sour acceuil. She is more thin and yellow than ever. Was able to assure her I had had a monstrously pleasant journey. Have wrote too much for one day. 'Tis Damnably Cold here.

*March 10th*

Coz. Charlotte is prodigiously disapproving of me, but Coz. Noll (Heaven bless him) makes very merry over my "amour" as he chooses to call my affair with Mr. A. When Cousin C.'s back is turned, he shouts in a jolly voice as large as his person, "Hey Miss, so you are enamoured of a Bad Bold Black Ancaster are you?"

"Yes, Coz. Noll," says I, "he is the pleasantest young man imaginable."

"Zounds!" says Coz. N. "I'll wager he isn't such a fine figure of a man as I was in my youth."

"Maybe not, but he is very handsome for all that, with the finest pair of Black Eyes and the most ravishing singing voice in Co. Down."

"Take care you Pert little Miss," says he, pulling me on his knee, "or the rascal will be seducing you next and then what will you do?" I begin to laugh at this but in comes Coz. Charlotte and I jump on to the floor, and am very busy smoothing out my petticoat, and poor Coz. Noll Hems and Haws and hurries into the garden!

Tom McMullan gave me a Black Rabbit in a cage to-day.

*March 11th*

'Tis as well Coz. Noll is such diverting company, for I

swear I never was in such an Intolerably Dull place. Am not astonished my three cousins married so soon. Apropos of this, Coz. C. has had a letter from Mary. She and her infants Leave for Dublin to-day. Coz. Charlotte scolds me day and night about my Immodest and Forward Behaviour, as she terms it, with regard to Mr. A. This morning in the Stillroom she said: "When I was a Girl, Miss, I had too much regard and esteem for my reputation" and so on in the same strain till I replied (somewhat pertly), "Perhaps Ma'am no young gentleman ever tried to break into *your* room!" Swear I think very ill of young women to be rude to their Elderly Relatives, but Coz. C. is so prodigiously tiresome sometimes that I cannot keep my feelings to myself.

For the rest, I pass my day in an insipid manner. I walk in the grounds and pick flowers, feed my Rabbit, sit at my tambour and embroider (very ill). I play on the spinnet and in the evening I play piquet with my two Cousins. There is not a new or diverting book in the house, and not a Masculine Form to be seen excepting Coz. Noll and the servants. If Papa hopes this enforced dulness will make me repent of my affair with Mr. A. he is greatly deceived. A few weeks of Coz. Charlotte's company, and I shall be ready to open my window to the next young gentleman who has an inclination to enter.

### March 12th

A highly agitating day. This morning as I was sitting on a log in the wood picking Primroses (these flowers grow in marvellous profusion here), I heard a familiar voice in my ear. Glanced up and near screamed at seeing Mr. Ancaster standing beside me and gazing at me in the most Ardent Manner Imaginable.

Happily I had the good sense to remain silent. If we had been discovered by Coz. C. Heaven only knows what would have happened. While I was attempting to collect my wits, he catched me in his arms and embraced me in the most Passionate Manner, pulling down my dress and kissing my neck and shoulders, till my first delight turned to something like alarm. I struggled to free myself, and an onlooker might have been pardoned for supposing he was my Assasin rather than my Lover. I was prepared to reproach him bitterly for his violent conduct, but unluckily for my dignity perceived suddenly that the powder from my head had whitened his cloth coat, giving him a Most Ludicrous Appearance, and I broke into a fit of merriment. This he took very ill, calling me a Flirt and a Capricious Heartless Slut, and Lord knows what else besides. Have observed before now that a man in love is the most Pompous Animal on this earth.

He looked so handsome in his rage, his Black Insolent Eyes flashing fire at me, that I could not bear to provoke him any longer and we sat down side by side among the flowers, as affable as two lambs. The Bold Wretch hearing of my banishment had followed me to Ballywiticock with the firm intention of winning me once and for all. We sat together very comfortable for several hours, till I heard Cousin C.'s voice calling me from the house. Before permitting me to leave him Mr. A. exhorted me to elope with him. "No," I cried, "this is not a matter to be decided all at once like buying a yard of watered tabby or a new gown." In short I am to have till the day after to-morrow to decide my fate. He will wait for me in the grounds and have a Chaise at the gates. Where we are then to go or what do Heaven best knows, for I dare swear Mr. A. does not. Was ever a poor female in a more distressful situation?

My inclination is to go—my prudence bids me stay but Lud! if one listen to prudence one might die a Spinster!

## *March 13th*

Am in a great state on Account of this Elopement. I change colour every time Coz. C. speaks to me, and I dare swear Coz. Noll who is as skilled in "affairs de coeur" as any man in Ireland suspects something. To tell the truth, I am not over sure if Mr. A.'s intentions are Honourable or not. That he is madly enamoured I do not doubt, but whether my coach ride to-morrow is to lead to the Altar or merely to a bed in an Inn is a matter I am not so easy about. 'Twould be Highly Indelicate for me to show my doubts to Mr. A., and I could scarcely say as I stepped into the Chaise, "By the by, Sir, I hope you are not trying to ruin me," yet the more I think of it, the more I recollect the fact that amidst all his passionate love Making the magical word "marriage," so dear to the heart of every young unwedded female, did not once occur! Now I come to consider it, he has more the air of a Lover than a possible Husband. Indeed the Ancasters are commonly supposed to have added to the population of Down more than any other family in the county. A pretty fool indeed I should look if I lost my reputation at 19 for the first handsome young man that made eyes at me!

## *March 14th*

Am decided to leave with my Lover this evening. Cannot abide the dulness of this house a moment longer. What is more, I am unable to communicate with Mr. A., not knowing where he lodges and having no person I could trust with a message. Am therefore bound to meet him to-night in the drive. If I were to fail him, he would be more than likely to pull me out of the house by force, and then we should have a duel between him and Coz. Noll, High Strikes from Coz. C. and lord knows what else besides!

Cannot think what baggage to take with me on this amorous little adventure. Have need of my jewels in case, as is more than probable, Mr. A. lacks Means, but am in a mighty fix with my Gowns. Suppose 'tis more Prudent to travel on an Elopement unencumbered by too much luggage, yet find it hard to make a wise selection of clothes. 'Tis unlikely I shall have any occasion for my blue Brocade gown with the gold embroidery, for example, but 'twould be a cruel wrench to part from it, for I dare swear I might go a hundred miles before I found a Gown that became me better. Wish I could have Betsy to help me, but the Hussey is the greatest talker living and cannot be trusted with a secret of such Vast Importance. There is also the matter of a letter to my father, praying him not to fall instantly into an Apoplectick Fit. I pray Heaven I am not making a great fool of myself over this affair. 'Tis monstrous what havoc a pair of Fine Dark Eyes will make in a susceptible female heart!

*March 15th*

To my vast amazement I am still here unwedded and unseduced! Truly it would seem as if Heaven Itself disapproved of Mr. A. for a more prodigious series of accidents than occurred last night can hardly be imagined. For a start Cousin C., who is accustomed most nights to retire to her bed at 10 o'clock, most unaccountably took it into her head to sit conversing with me till 11 o'clock, the very hour of my Rendezvous. In vain I fidgeted, yawned and feigned fatigue, the more she talked as if the Deuce Itself was inspiring her to provoke me.

At every sound outside the window I broke into a cold sweat, thinking 'twas at least Mr. A. preparing to rush in and carry me away, like a second Rape of the Sabines. At length my old tormentor consented to retire, and I was free to complete my preparations for flight in the solitude of my bed chamber. In a mighty bustle I clapped on my Travelling Gown, then discovered to my utter confusion that my cloak and hood were all in pieces, left thus by that idle slut Betsy who had been altering its shape in the afternoon and had been so Lazy as to leave it all unsewn. A pretty business I had stitching it together in some sort of fashion, all the time picturing to myself poor Mr. A. waiting for me in the grounds in a very Frenzy of Impatience. Then down I hastened below, and placed a note for Coz. Noll in the library—was then highly vexed to find I had left my jewel box behind. Up I ran again, and resolved to leave the house now dead or alive, prepared to creep down the stairs. By a Monstrous stroke of Ill Luck, I stumbled in the dark against a table ladened with china which Coz. C. chooses to keep for ornament on the landing. A great upset, and the precious plates and pots rolled downstairs with a clatter that would have waked the Dead. Heard a cry of "Thief, Thief," from Cousin C.'s room, and I had scarcely time to bundle myself box and all under the table, before the Lady appeared in person followed by Coz. N. in his Nightcap, with a candle in one Hand and a Blunderbuss in the other. Lay all of quake under the table, praying Heaven I should not be discovered. A great to do. Cousin Charlotte weeping over her broken crockery, Coz. Noll pulling open the presses and roaring, "Come out with thee, Villain, or I'll blow thy brains out." By amazing good Fortune, the thought of looking beneath the table did not occur to them. To my Vast consternation indeed, Coz. C. displayed an inclination to enter my room and wake me, but Coz. N. with his customary good nature told her to leave me in peace.

Finding no trace of a Thief, my Cousins retired to their rooms, putting the blame for the traccasserie on the Cat. I thanked my stars that all was safely over. I emerged from my hiding place, ran below and climbed out into the

garden by the library window, which I contrived to un-
fasten without much pain.

'Twas raining outside and plaguey dark, and Gemini!
what were my feelings in finding when I arrived at my
Rendezvous not a trace of my Lover or Chaise or any
damned thing! I sat down in the rain and drizzle and wept
for sheer melancholy. Yet I could not blame Mr. A. Doubtless he had waited impatiently for my coming, and seeing
no sign of me, concluded bitterly that I had repented of my
decision. There was naught for me to do but retire to my
room in deep dejection of spirits and chilled to the bone.
This morning as I dressed (after a sleepless night) it flashed
upon me all on a sudden that my Note to Coz. Noll was
still on the library table! Though I was only in a Petticoat
and my hair loose, I ran below as fast as I could go. Was
just in time, for Coz. Noll was standing with the cursed
letter in his hand. Snatched it from him, and hurled it in
the fire to his vast amazement.

He gazed at me curiously, then remarked, "Your conduct Miss, is very strange, 'pon my word. Am I right in
supposing that you left this note, intended evidently for my
perusal, on this table last night?"

To which I replied with a low curtsey, "Sir, there are
many things done by night which one repents of next morning, as no doubt you yourself have often found to your Cost!"

He laughed heartily at this and called me a "Sly little
Cat," and said no more on the matter. Coz. C. has been
sick all day of a Vapour, the result of last night's disturb-
ances. Asked whether I had heard any sounds, was constrained to lie to my vast regret.

My hand is nearly off have wrote so much.


*March 17th*

No word from Mr. A. I fear he is highly Enraged
against me!

## *March 18th*

To Church with Coz. Noll and Coz. C. Dr. Mahon preached a sermon to us on David and Bathsheba and the Beauty of Chastity, which I took to heart. Am firmly resolved to think no more of the opposite Sex. I swear if I had been Mr. A. I would have waited another hour before going off in a Passion.

## *March 19th*

Returned to Castle Kearney, bearing a sealed letter from Cousin Charlotte. Could guess too well that it contained something Odious about me, but could not open it. My father greeted me with a trifle more amiability than he had vouchsafed to show me on parting, but has still a certain severity in his manner towards me. Ned in great high feather having shot three seals this morning. He had the impudence to express a hope that my visit to Ballywiticock had had a chastening effect upon me, for which piece of Forwardness I slapped his face. 'Tis a pity he is such a monstrously discreet, virtuous Paragon of a young man, else he would be attractive enough. If he had one Foible and not so many Forts he would be more tolerable.

I delivered Cousin C.'s letter to Papa to-night, and hastened from the room to escape any consequences which might ensue. What can Mr. A. be about? Not a word from him. Could anything exceed the fickleness of these men?

## *March 20th*

Am in Disgrace once more judging from my father's and Ned's severe glances. What have I done to offend again? It suddenly occurs to me that Cousin Charlotte had by some Devilish means or other discovered my attempt at

elopement. 'Tis more than likely that Coz. Noll has blabbed
to her of my note. He has never been able to keep his own
love affairs from her so, 'tis not likely that he has been
able to keep mine.

At all events I am being treated with as much severity
as if I had indeed committed a faux pas with Mr. A.,
which shows plainly that Virtue is not its own Reward.

Spent half the day baking bread with Betsy.

### *March 21st*

To-day rode over to Mara on my dear Juno, to take old
Mrs. M'Culla a pie and some wine. The old dame declares
she is Dying, but, as Paddy, who accompanied me, remarked, she has been in that condition for years. Should
not be astounded if she out-lived us all.

Victor slew 2 ducks to-day, and Papa declares he will
beat him if he does not mend his ways.

### *March 22nd*

My father called me to his study this morning, and com-
municated to me a most amazing piece of intelligence. We
are to set off next month for a Grand Tour of Europe,
visiting first my sister Foley and her husband in Derbyshire, proceeding from thence to London and the Continent. My father offered as his reason for this sudden decision his earnest desire that Ned and me should see more
of the World than is possible in this uncivilized country,
and thus be enabled to enlarge and cultivate our minds. I
own that at first the prospect of this Trip and all the many
Pleasures 'twould bring in its train filled me with delight.
Then I realised that poor Mr. A. would most certainly
not be permitted to accompany me on this journey, and
my eyes filled with tears.

Would I meet any young man more handsome in all the

capitals of Europe? Would the sight of the finest Churches and palaces be more agreeable to me than a loving glance from his Wicked black eyes? Plainly no.

I proceeded to lay these objections before my parent, thanking him for his great kindness in offering me this delectable and costly excursion, but confessing that Love most hardhearted of taskmasters, kept me rooted to my native soil. This avowal threw my father into a Perfect Fury. He became completely scarlet in the face and broke into a string of oaths committing both me and Mr. A., whom he described as a Damned Profligate to utter perdition. He appealed to Highest Heaven to know why he had been cursed with such a frail, foolish, insolent, wilful slut as a daughter, asked me if I was set on dragging my good name and honour in the dust, and finally assured me that he would beat me Black and Blue if I ever dared mention Mr. A. again in his hearing.

He seized his crop at these words, and brandished it so alarmingly that I burst out weeping. This calmed him as I have observed it never fails to do, and he patted me on the Head with some signs of contrition and told me to go and mop my eyes, adding that the Lord knew why one of his Progeny was a civil young man of such good dispositions and the other a baggage and hellcat like me. To which I replied: "Maybe sir, Ned takes after dear Mama, while I have inherited your nature." Then ran away in great haste. Had to resort to my smelling bottle. Parental Anger and Disappointed Love has made me tremble in every limb. Made myself a roguish cap with lavender ribbons.

### March 24th

All here in a prodigious bustle in preparation for this Tour. My father closeted day and night with the Steward. Indeed I own I have my doubts as to how the Estate will fare, once his vigilant eye is removed. Even now I have known the tenants remove the gates for firewood under our very noses, and as for killing our pigeons and attempting to sell them at our kitchen door, 'tis the commonest thing in the world.

I suspect that Ned, by the anxiety he shows to procure for himself an Elegant outfit for this same trip, has hopes of some amorous adventures on our travels. Doubtless he hopes by the means of velvet coats and other fripperies to play the part of a beau and to gain the favours of some of the pretty little wantons who, from all accounts, abound like rabbits on the Continent. As for me I have decided to purchase my wardrobe in England. In this remote country there are few chances of setting oneself up elegantly in the way of clothes. I own I have no idea of what is worn at the present moment by women of Fashion in London, and must trust to my sister to advise me on the subject of head-dresses and gowns, else I shall make my debut in Town looking monstrously Rustick.

### March 27th

It seems that the Coach is in a great state of delapidation. Ned and me have begged Papa to have it painted in a genteel colour for our Voyage.

I was much put out last night at being informed by my father that I am not to have Betsy with me on this Trip. Mrs. Stewart, in old days maid to dear Mama and Governess to Ned and me (I can recollect now her unavailing attempts to instil the rudiments of Writing and the Holy Scriptures into our obdurate infant minds), is, it would seem, living in Newry since her Widowhood, and is to combine in her person the offices of duenna and Abigail. From what I recollect of her she is an excellent amiable female, but will not to my mind replace the ministrations of my little Betsy, who, with all her faults of indiscretion and talkativeness, is I truly believe devoted to my interests.

Besides she is highly accomplished in the arts of dress-making, hairdressing and rouging. The poor Wretch broke into fearful lamentations on hearing of my parent's decision. She was somewhat comforted at being presented with an elegant cap trimmed with cherry ribbons.

## April 1st

To-day being April Fool's Day, I played a silly little jest at poor Ned's expense. He has lately taken to Snuff, and I contrived to sprinkle a small quantity of pepper in his box which threw him into a frenzy of sneezing, and made Papa and me laugh till we nearly split.

## April 9th

I have not wrote in this book for several days all being very busy here. The weather of late has been prodigiously fine, and the woods and gardens full of sweet smelling flowers have enticed me from my books and Pen.

My father returned from Belfast, where he has been these last two days on affairs, brings back with him a diverting and ludicrous little book entitled "The Traveller's Aid", which is designed to warn and advise those about to set out on a journey. If half that is contained in it is true, our hopes of reaching London safe and sound are less than nothing. If we are happy enough to escape from highwaymen, footpads, thiefs and murderous landlords, we will doubtless die of consumption contracted by lying between damp sheets in an Inn.

Though containing much that is foolishly alarming and extravagant, this same book offers some wise cautions on the matter of travelling well armed and well provided with dry and clean bedclothes, which I believe will be of assistance to us in our peregrinations. Profound silence reigns with regard to Mr. A. Can his Love have changed to cruel indifference?

*April 20th*

Yesterday we held a great dinner for the Tenants. My
father and Ned sat at one table with the men whilst I
entertained the females at another. Many speeches were
made testifying to the Love and Esteem in which our
family is held by its dependants. Many toasts were drunk,
and the food was plentiful, among other items being veal,
chickens, ducks, ham and pigeon pie, tarts and custard.
Dancing and other sports continued in the courtyard, with
loud sounds of Merrymaking, long after I had retired to
bed. I should not be astonished if we heard of some broken
heads and black eyes to-day. From the looks that Paddy,
John and Tommy McSwinney were casting at Rose Quinn,
Mary McMullan and Jane Black respectively, I am also
apprehensive that this Fete will lead to some birthdays!

*April 26th*

To-day is my last in my dear Home. I own I cannot contemplate parting from this place where I have spent my
Childhood without some melancholy. Events have also
proved that Mr. A. is still enamoured of me, and this
makes me still more reluctant to depart. Last night, when I
was taking the air in the Rose Garden, a small Ragged
boy approached me and presented me with a little box,
then hastily making his departure. Opening it with a beat-
ing Heart, I perceived inside a small but graceful Locket
encrusted with brilliants, and containing 2 locks of hair
bound together with blue ribbon. These I recognised with
deep Emotion, the blacker as belonging to Mr. A. and the
other as being a piece of my own hair which I had once
had the complaisance to grant him. With this gift was a
morsel of paper inscribed in my beloved's hand, "Forget
me not, D.A." My feelings overcame me at the thought
of seeing no more my wicked dear Ancaster and having

no longer the pleasure of hearing my favourite Ballads sung to me in his fine manly voice, and I sat for some time in tears. Must own however that my feelings of natural regret are mingled with triumph and relief that I am still the Mistress of David Ancaster's wayward Heart.

The great bustle we are in for to-morrow's start enables me somewhat to forget my unhappy Love affair. I swear I cannot think how we shall be able to arrange our Monstrous amount of luggage in the Coach. My father who regards the "Traveller's Aid" as a Second Gospel, has in obedience to its dictates furnished himself with the following articles, and no amount of Persuasion from Ned or me will move him, Viz. :

A Portfolio case of instruments for Writing.
A Sketch book and a Note Book.
An Opera Glass.
A Tinder Box.
A Night Lamp.
Sheets and a Quilt.
A Mariner's Compass in a snuff box.
A Thermometer and tooth pick in a cane.
A Barometer in a sword.
A Blunderbuss and a case of Pistols.

This, added to Ned's vast wardrobe, my own garments and sundry articles such as Prayer Books, Stays, ornaments, comfit boxes, fans, purses to saying nothing of Mrs. Stewart and the Valets' belongings will laden us up, till we can scarcely move.

Bade my dogs, horses, geese, the black Rabbit and my two dear Goats a loving farewell. Shall retire to-night with Mr. A.'s gift next my Heart—Faute de Mieux !

*April 27th*

Made an early start in a fine soft rain. The servants

(indoor and out), headed by the Steward, and Betsy in tears with a Bouquet of flowers, bade us a melancholy adieu from the Castle Gates. I'll own I think we made a magnificent show, the coach being newly painted, the 6 horses as fresh as daisies, the Valets and Paddy in new livery, and Papa, Ned, me and Mrs. S. in elegant travelling attire.

The road from Kearney to Ballybangor was all a-buzz with tenants. The cottagers came to their doors and wished us God Speed with smiles, waving of hands and curtseys. Old Mrs. McSwinney had the Boldness to exclaim as we passed her, "I make no doubt, Miss Cleone, you'll be forgetting your black Ancaster and bringing back a fine Husband," which piece of Impudence made me blush from head to foot.

The roads in a mighty bad state and the country looking somewhat melancholy in the wet. My mind occupied with tender thoughts of Mr. A., so did not heed the jolting which else I should have found intolerable.

Dined and changed horses at Newtown. Reached Belfast at night. Am mortally stiff and weary! This inn is as Filthy as any I have been in.

### April 28th

Spent a vastly Uneasy night reclining in a chair in a wrapper, my feet on another chair, the bed being too miserably dirty for my taste. Was also loath to disturb the Fleas and Cockroaches who seemed to have made it their habitation.

Was woke up very early by a street cry below my window of *Dirty Butter for Servants!* and putting my head out of window, perceived that 'twas a wet cold day. We were all mightily vexed to learn that the Pacquet which is to convey us to Liverpool with half a dozen other passengers cannot put out to sea to-day, and so we may find ourselves in this odious place till such time as Heaven is pleased to send us a fair Wind. Indeed I have heard of Pacquets sailing as much as 23 days after the time advertised.

This town is not more lively than when I last visited it; though well built enough 'tis a dull place in my opinion, and I pray Heaven we shall not be long in it.

I ventured out in a hood with Mrs. S., but found to my amazement that Unwatered Tabby is 10/6 a yard at the best mercers here and poor stuff at that. To Ned and my father's disgust, the Company in this Inn is comprized solely of Linen merchants. Decent enough looking men in my opinion, but Ned turns up his Nose when they enter the room, and exclaims in a none too low voice, "S'death, open the window, I smell flax" for which piece of coxcombry I reproached him.

My father mightily pleased this afternoon to meet Colonel N——t in the yard. He is up in Belfast on the matter of selling a mare.

It seems, among other pieces of country gossip, that Lady B—— is already weary of Lord B——'s society (he has no ideas in his head beyond playing Backgammon), that Coz. Noll, poor soul, was caught by Cousin C. kissing a pretty milkmaid in the dairy; and from the South, that a Judge in Dublin who had some hot words with a barrister offered to meet him in a few minutes when he had put off his wig and gown, which shows how much Duelling is now the Mode.

### April 30th

I take up my Pen to record a most Agitating incident which occurred this morning at breakfast. My father and I were sitting at table when I chanced to glance up and saw to my utter Confusion sitting opposite us no less a person than Mr. A. his eyes fixed on me with the coolest smile imaginable. If it had been the Devil himself, I could

not have been more astonished. My first thought was to
prevent my father observing him, but he saw me change
colour and looked up also. Mr. A. bowed without turning
a hair. Followed a terrible silence. My Heart almost jumped
clean out of my Body. Mr. Ancaster rose slowly and
advancing towards us in a leisurely manner said: "Permit
me, sir, to have the honour of wishing you both a pleasant
journey." "Damn your impertinence, you young Puppy,"
roared my father in a Fury, rising and drawing his sword,
and would, I believe, have slain him on the spot; but Mr.
A., still with calm insolence, waved him back and said
affably, "Pray, sir, do not make a scene in a public inn.
Also as you are, I understand, about to set off on what may
be a rough sea voyage, I should advise you to keep quiet
after meals unless of course you are blessed with a strong
stomach." Then turning to me and dropping his bantering
air, he seized my hand and kissed it with the ardent words,
"Farewell, adorable Cleone. Remain faithful to me," and
dashed from the room. I ran to the window, and hanging
out of it to the vast amazement of the onlookers, was
exactly in time to throw Mr. A. a kiss as he galloped at
neck-break speed from the yard. My father meanwhile
swearing terribly, and transfixed by Wrath to his chair. I
then swooned, this seeming to me the only means of escape
from an Embarrassing Situation.

Ned and my father have been out all to-day, so thank
Heaven I have not been obliged to face them. What their
Feelings are, I can guess too well. Mrs. S. very solicitous
for me and says, "poor Darling Dear, I don't wonder at
your being taken by such a Sweet young Gentleman. When
I was a young Thing I was the same. A pair of black eyes
or a neat pair of legs would send me clean out of my
senses."

Pray Heaven our boat may sail soon. Every stock and
stone of this wretched country reminds me of Mr. A. and
drives me near crazy with Frustrated Love.

# DERBYSHIRE

*May 5th—Fulford Hall*

I own I had doubts as to whether my gowns would be very dowdy, but I had no notion of the extent to which the Fashions in England are in advance of our provincial Irish Modes.

Cary indeed declares that I shall be in need of a complete New wardrobe before I am fit to appear in Town. The Sacque it would seem is all the Mode, but Hoops are no longer worn so big. Skirts are longer and more elaborate. In short, the elegant form must protrude a trifle behind, as well as on the Hips. Heads are worn now as Big as one can bear them, and are decorated so Cary declares in Town with Ships, Gardens and other Fantasies. The Calash is from all accounts much thought of for travelling and for this thank Heaven, for I have a very pretty new one, and 'tis a Mode that becomes me Vastly well.

Cary is pleased to say that I have grown into a Fine Beautiful girl. She is to take the matter of my gowns into her own hands, and among other items, we have already decided on a quilted petticoat in pale rose, with a brocade overgown of the same shade (a trifle deeper), and for day wear a plain dress of brown silk with gold embroidery. Cary is good enough to give me a new gown of Spitalfields silk most elegantly embroidered in Flowers, which is too narrow for her figure at present. With it I am to wear a lace cap my hair being worn plain. What with this question of clothes, my pleasure at seeing Cary after so many years and her two children (the prettiest infants possible), and the vast strangeness of this English life, I have been in a prodigious Bustle with neither the time or the inclination to write in this Journal. Indeed for a day on our arrival I was utterly prostrate, my strength being quite exhausted by a violent Tossing of 36 hours in the Channel; (the high Seas burst open our cabin window and near drowned Mrs. S. and self), and the fatigues of our land journey which though uneventful was tedious by reason of the bad Roads.

We lay in Cheshire at Mr. Ingram's, to whom my father had letters of recommendation and indeed I believe if it had not been for the hot gruels given me by his good lady I should have Expired, so weak had my violent Sickness left me.

The country round here is wild and beautiful with crags and woods and waterfalls, yet to my mind England, however blessed with natural advantages, is Insipid compared with Ireland. I think the Inhabitants contribute to this effect, for they have a clean busy air about them, as if they loved Work and were anxious to do their duty. This place is a very fine Mansion house constructed of deep red brick and situated pleasantly with woods at its back and smooth lawns in front sloping down to a small stream. Its terrace, walks and gardens are Trimmer and Neater than anything I could imagine—not a grass or stone appears to be out of place, and I truly believe the flowers are so Orderly that they dare not drop their petals on the Sward. The very yews are clipped in an exact manner so that they scarcely seem to be living trees. The kitchen garden is well stocked with fruit trees, flowers and vegetables, while near it is a Poultry yard, whose inhabitants are under my sister's care. Nothing more unlike our wild and beautiful Kearney could be imagined, yet I will own 'tis beautiful in its own fashion, and Cary has reason to be proud of being the Mistress of such a noble Estate.

My sister who is shortly expecting to be brought to bed, and lives in fervent hopes that this addition to her family will not prove another female, appears to have found Tom an agreeable husband, judging by her blooming appearance and constant praises of his Kindness and consideration. This morning I assisted her in feeding her Fowls, and she broached the subject of Mr. A. and my unfortunate Love for him. I must own I was agreeably surprised at the amiable and affectionate manner in which she spoke, having been accustomed to receive little but curses and Disapproving glances from my Family on this same matter of late. In her opinion Mr. A., though doubtless somewhat of a Wild Rake at present, has an excellent Heart and would make me an amiable husband. Netherless she thinks it a good thing that we should be parted for a year or so, to prove whether our Love is of an enduring kind or merely the result of Unbridled Passion. To tell the truth, I do not care much whether our Love is unbridled or not, so long as we are permitted to satisfy it. Once Wed to Mr. A. I can promise to keep him faithful to me!

### May 7th

This morning was woke up early by the cawing of rooks, and throwing open my window perceived that it was a fine fresh day. Felt quite recovered from the fatigues of my journey and had regained my Natural Liveliness of spirits. Threw on some garments, and made my way below into the garden, singing in a Lusty voice to the vast amazement of a garden boy who gazed at me doubtless thinking I was out of my mind. The Beauty of the scene, the dew on flower and bush sparkling in the early sun, the joyous Warbling of the birds, produced a most exhilarating effect on me, and I spent an agreeable half hour in the wood picking violets and carving the initials D.A., so dear to me, on a tree with the aid of a little silver pen knife.

On returning to the house, I found my sister with my little nieces on the terrace, just preparing to send the Footman in search of me. It would seem that the chamber-maid, come to wake me with a cup of chocolate was mightily surprised at finding my bed empty, concluded immediately that I had eloped over night, and so my absence had caused a little stir in the household. I laughed to myself to see how nine years of marriage to an English husband has changed my sister's disposition. One could scarcely recognise in this genteel and staid young matron, the capricious and vivacious girl who was used, as I remember well, to ride round the field before breakfast, attired in nothing but a chemise.

My father, Tom and Ned watching bull baiting in the village after breakfast. Cary and self to Derby in the post chaise to visit the Mantua Maker. The roads pretty bad but good enough after Ireland. Was again impressed by the neatness of the countryside. The village which adjoins the House is as clean as if it were washed out everyday. The villagers very profuse in their Salutations as we passed through, all being tenants, and Tom their Magistrate into the bargain.

By the Bowling Green, we passed the Parson, a decent enough man Cary says when he is not in Liquor, but married to a low serving wench. All looked curiously at self.

During our drive my sister took on her to inform me that I must guard against speaking with too strong an Irish accent, unless I wished to appear Provincial and Uncouth. I own I was foolishly vexed at this and said bridling that, "Indeed, Ma'am, Mr. Ancaster had always considered my voice the most agreeable charm I possessed," to which she replied laughing, " 'Tis not a question, Miss, of Beauty, but of Elegance." She then proceeded to say that while we were on the subject of Mr. A., she trusted that I would not allow my Infatuation for him to stand in my way if any other Likely young Gentleman were to ask for my hand. "For," she said smilingly, "without Flattery you have grown into a very lovely little wretch, my dear sister" adding that a marriage based on Mutual Esteem often proved as happy as a more Passionate union.

These arguments did not move me at all, my heart being as firmly attached to my lover after this last week as it ever was. My sister however spoke with such good nature and so evident a desire for my Welfare that her remarks did not in any way vex me. Indeed I have often observed that a woman who is wedded to a man she Esteems is always more amiable to Unmarried Females than a lady whose nuptials have proved unhappy, though why this should be I cannot explain.

Arrived at Derby, a fine town, we went to the Mantua maker and were closeted with her for several hours, our talk being all of taffety, lute strings, sacks, stays and handkerchiefs.

Dined with Lady Chicheley, an acquaintance of my sister, a tall blonde woman not very young with a Haughty manner and a sharp tongue. She spoke with contempt of the County Society, declaring that she near died of Ennui when compelled to live out of town. All this in a Mincing voice, with monstrous twirling of her fan and a searching Quizzing scrutiny of my person. Amongst other things she mentioned Sir Charles Mills as being the only young man in her opinion of any Breeding or Easiness of Manners in Derbyshire. Inquired of my sister if she did not think Miss Charlotte Holt had grown marvellously stout these days. "I should not be surprised," says she with a malicious glance, "if we had one of those Hasty marriages between her and a certain young gentleman we know of"; then later to my sister, "I dare swear dear ma'am you are all of a tremble in case you should present Mr. Foley with another female. Lud! what a Calamity 'twould be to have three girls to marry off when they are grown, and no son to inherit such a fine place." In short I was not sorry when we took our leave of her. My sister, who was not looking

over Pleased, remarked in the Chariot that Lady C. was not
cared for much in Derbyshire, and the county wished that
she would take her airs and scandalous Tongue to London
and keep them there for good and all. "They say," my
sister said, winking at me, "that the lady was highly vexed
when hoops were no longer the Mode. I can well believe it.
Doubtless she found them convenient to hide her lovers
under. She is a bad woman, sister."

By the Assembly Hall in Full Street, a young man
elegantly dressed, with a fair complexion observed us and
bowed low to Cary, meanwhile fixing his eye on me in a
Coy way. After some minutes conversation we drove on.
My sister informed me that he was Sir Charles Mills, the
richest young man in Derbyshire, "and handsome into the
Bargain you can't deny that", with a searching glance at
me. To which I replied that he was well enough, but that
to tell the truth I had not observed him very closely.

*May 8th*

To-day coming down to breakfast noticed a young
Female, poorly but neatly clad, standing in the Hall, her
eyes red and swollen with weeping and tears running down
her cheeks. Not knowing the reason for her Grief, I handed
her my cambric handkerchief and passed on into the
breakfast room. While we were in the middle of taking tea,
my brother in law joined us with a severe and thoughtful
countenance. I inquired of him who the weeping girl was,
whereupon he explained that she was the daughter of the
blacksmith. She had been Indiscreet enough to permit herself to be seduced, and now has had a child to the vast indignation so it would seem of the Village (though how it
concerns them Lord knows). The poor wanton is sent to my
brother as Magistrate, and should so he says be sent to the
House of Correction (or Bridewell as 'tis called in this
country), but he has had pity on the poor slut and has

punished her with nothing more than a severe Admonition and many questions as to who the father is. This she refuses to say, except that he is a very grand Gentleman and will provide for his child. Could one believe that such a prodigious To Do would be made about this unlucky *faux pas*, for I could see by merely looking at her that she is at heart a virtuous female? Poor wretch if she was a Lady of Fashion she could have 10 bastards without turning a hair, but being of low birth and doubtless envied in the Village for her superior charms, she is reviled and persecuted.

## *May 10th*

Lud! I have something to record to-day. Caught Ned kissing the Prettiest chamber maid in the Linen room! I felt it my Duty to warn him that licentiousness of all kinds is looked on very severely in this country, and unless he wishes the girl to end in the Bridewell, he had better leave her alone. This he took very badly, flying into a passion and telling me to mind my own damned affairs. I think Papa would be astonished to hear this, but thank Heaven I have the Generosity to hold my Tongue.

## *May 11th*

We made an agreeable excursion to-day to some Ruins not far from here. Tom, my father, Ned, me and Sir Charles Mills who was of our party, on horseback. Cary, the infants and Mrs. Dixie in the Chaise. I own I was glad to have this opportunity of showing off my new Riding Suit, which is richly laced and excessively elegant, and I think shows my figure off to advantage. Our route lay through very pretty country, but to tell the truth I was too occupied in receiving the attentions of Sir Charles who never left my side to pay very much attention to the Scenery.

When we arrived at our destination, a very fine Ivy clad Ruin situated beautifully by a waterfall, a slight commotion was caused when my new plumed hat was blown from my head and down a cascade, where it caught on a rock.

Sir Charles with great gallantry instantly climbed down among the rocks and spray in pursuit of it, delivering it to me with a glance so full of Ardour and so low a Bow that the Company smiled knowingly at each other.

We dined at Mrs. Egerton's House. She is a young and pretty Widow, and shows her grief for her late departed lord in a prodigious display of black gowns, black caps, black gloves and sealing Wax, and so on; but I dare swear she will soon console herself by the manner in which she ogled Ned the second he set foot in the house. Ned highly flattered by her attentions.

All the county it seems talking of the death of Squire Russel of these parts, who was a Strange person from all accounts. He drove his chaise with Straw Reins, had a boxing match with a highwayman and beat him, and when he lay dying had a cock fight in his chamber. Cary declares that she met him once in Derby at the Virgins Inn, attired in a suit of sacking. Yet they say we Irish are Crazy!

### May 12th

My Birthday. Received fine gifts from all my family, viz. a Gilt edged Prayer book from Papa and a Pearl Ornament, a sweet gown of Sprigged Muslin from Cary, an elegant riding crop from Tom, a bracelet from Ned, and a blue stoll worked by my Nieces.

Sir Charles rode over after breakfast on a fine grey mare. I own he looked Well enough in his riding suit.

Invited me out to the garden to admire the flowers. On our way through the Hall we passed the young female I have before mentioned, who was waiting on Tom again. She gave a mighty jump at seeing him and cast him a piteous look. Sir C. changed colour at the sight of her, frowned and hurried me into the garden, from which hints of embarrassment I concluded instantly that he was her betrayer. I fixed him sternly with my Eye and said, "That poor girl has narrowly escaped the house of Correction. I hope her betrayer," then paused, "whoever he may be, will provide for her and her Infant," to which he answered with a smile, "Dear ma'am for your Sweet Sake I promise he will be generous," and no more was said on the matter. Sir C. stayed to dinner, took tea with us, and not having left us in the evening was invited to stay for supper which he did with great eagerness. After our meal, I played Handel on the Harpsichord and he sat so close that his cheek was almost on my shoulder. He never removed his eyes, the colour of Blue china, from my face unless to glance at my hands. I dare swear he has not really an Ear for music, for when I struck a discord by accident and glanced at him he gave me a smile of Delight and said, "Odsbodikins, you play divinely, Ma'am," and this without a trace of Sarcasm. Indeed I think the English are the most Pompous People imaginable. Showing no desire to depart, my sister must needs ask him to lie the night here, and so a room is being prepared for him.

### May 13th

Hanging out of my window this morning in my night-shift I looked down and perceived Sir C., his eyes fixed on my bare shoulders with an ardent smile, upon which I drew in Modestly.

He left shortly after breakfast, promising to see me again at the Assembly Ball to-morrow. To Church. The Sermon so Lengthy I near fell asleep. Mrs. Stewart came to me with great complaints. It seems that she and Mrs. Wilkens, the housekeeper here, have had some words together on the matter of the best recipe for ginger preserve, and

Mrs. W. so far forgot herself as to stick out her tongue at Mrs. S. Mrs. S. said some bitter things about England and the English in general, but I have bound her over to keep the Peace.

## *May 15th*

Last evening Ned and me and Cary went by Coach to the Assembly at Derby. Wore my rose Brocade, Very Magnificent. My hair dressed up high with handfuls of horse hair and pins. 'Twas powdered, curled and dressed with feathers and flowers. Felt somewhat Agitated at finding myself in the Assembly Room, surrounded by a prodigious crowd of gentlemen and ladies in elegant attire. Was presented by my sister to Lady Ferrers the patroness, who was pleased to compliment Cary on my appearance.

This same lady complained that the Assemblies had been so ill managed by the late patroness, ladies being permitted to dance in long aprons, and even Attorneys Clerks and Shopkeepers being admitted against the rules, that the attendance had greatly diminished. She said, "I fear that some of the Misses may find themselves without partners." Felt very melancholy as I heard these words, more especially as I perceived Lady Chicheley, in a gown cut so low that one blushed to see her, watching me with an air of malice. I own I was Delighted when I saw Sir Charles making his way towards me, and so close did he keep to me all the evening that I did not miss a dance, though I observed several other Ladies obliged to dance together which to my mind is a Sad sight, and speaks very ill for Derbyshire gallantry. Sir C. set his Heart on partnering me in Cotillion, Country Dance and Minuet. The latter to my mind is a tedious affair. Lady C. looked daggers at me. Doubtless furious to see her lover so Catched by me. To bed, very weary after a long jolting ride home over odious rough roads.

## *May 16th*

Last night my sister had a large company to Supper, and indeed I had a very pretty lesson on the Manners and customs of these English. Among the guests were Sir Charles Mills, Sir John and Lady Chicheley, My lord and lady Ferrers, Mrs. Dixie, Mrs. Egerton, Lady Lucy Forsythe, Captain Bolton of the Dragoons and many others whose names I have forgot. I must have spent more than $2\frac{1}{2}$ hours over my Toilette, my sister having impressed upon me the necessity of looking my most elegant for this Distinguished gathering. Mrs. S. and my sister's maid were summoned to my assistance, and I must own that the result was very tolerable. Feel I must indeed note down my costume more fully, for a more Becoming one could not be imagined Viz. : a Sack dress of red brocade made low and tight in the bodice, completed by frills and fichus of finest Lace, worn over an open white satin dress and a white skirt very much frilled and caught up with Blue Love Knots. My hair, thank Heaven, was still dressed from the other night, and needed but a touch of powder and a few flowers to look highly elegant. I swear I would have given a fortune to have enabled Mr. A. to see me, for I wager in his wildest dreams he has never imagined me as pretty as I then appeared. 'Tis marvellous what wonders a Fashionable gown, to say nothing of Rouge and Pearl Powder will work, provided needless to say the figure and face are already Passable.

My sister, examining me, was highly satisfied with my appearance, only admonishing me to use my Fan gracefully, for said she, "There is a whole Language in the fan. With it the woman of fashion can express Disdain, Love, indifference, encouragement and so on." To tell the truth I had never thought of all this before, having found my eyes sufficient up to now to convey any message I wished to the other Sex.

The Supper was a very fine formal affair, though lacking in my opinion the joviality which distinguishes such gatherings in my native country. The excessive light of the candles, the loud conversation, which was all of such topics as Mr. Pitt's Gout, Death of Madame de Pompadour, and so on, and the wine which flowed like water, produced a certain drowsiness in me; but Sir Charles, who was placed next to me, seemed pleased enough with my conversation though I am convinced 'twas Foolish. The food was marvellously rich and plentiful, and the soups, fish, fowls, pies, chickens, jellies, cream, fruit and custards would have fed a small army. I thought tenderly of Mr. A. as I ate an Almond Pie for I remembered perfectly well that this is his favourite sweetmeat.

Lost £3 at whisk in the Drawing Room, where the Ladies retired leaving the Gentlemen to their wine. After several hours as there was no sign of the Gentlemen, and I had a pain in my head, I made my Adieux and slipt away. Passing the Supper Room I heard loud laughter and shouts and clanking of glass, which told me plainly enough why we had not had the pleasure of our male friends' society. All on a sudden the door opened and 2 Footmen emerged, bearing between them the Limp body of Sir Charles, his face flushed and swollen with excessive drinking! As I gazed at him I contracted a Sudden and perhaps unreasonable Distaste for him. His Inebriated condition exhibited more plainly the weak and debauched expression of his mouth and chin, which I had not noticed before. In short he presented a repulsive appearance. I hurried to make my way upstairs, but Captain Bolton, also very much in his Cups, staggered out after his friend, and catching sight of me reeled up the stairs in my Pursuit. We reached the landing in this way, where he caught hold of my dress and then my waist, saying in an odious Hoarse voice, "Dear sweet adorable little monster! I'm damned if I am not in Love with your beautiful Irish eyes. Let's to bed." My answer to this piece of Impudence was a sound Box on the Ears, which completely upset the gallant Dragoon, his Legs being as unsteady as his wits, and sent him falling against the wall. What happened then I cannot say, for I never stopped to look, retiring hastily to my room. I do not doubt he will hesitate before making advances of this kind to a Modest Irish Lady whom he has never even said a word to beyond "How d'ye do ma'am." In Ireland, we have our failings like any other nation, but Passionate Love, not mere Licentiousness, is usually the cause of our indiscretions. As for these Drunken Young Beaux, I remember with Pride **that Mr. A. with all his faults, has never been seen even** at a Race Ball, by my Eyes at all events, in anything more than a state of Lively Exhilaration. In short, he is able to take his wine as a Gentleman should.

### May 17th

To-morrow my father and Ned and I set off on our journey to London. I shall be sorry to part with Cary once more, and in all Honesty I do not Relish the idea of the many discomforts of travelling, the eternal jolting over bad roads, my Papa and Ned swearing and complaining when their legs became cramped, the filthy inn food or the chilly large bed in some stranger's house. This is a very agreeable place, and I am certain by Tomorrow evening I shall be regretting the easiness of my Four Poster here.

Went with Cary to visit an Almhouse which she interests herself in. Gave the old women a guinea to buy Snuff with. It would seem that the position of Squire's Lady in this country entails a Monstrous amount of good works, such as visiting and supporting alm houses and schools and so on. Cary has founded a spinning, knitting and sewing school for Penniless Girls, and all this not from particular Love of the Tenants, whom I suspect she finds tedious after our lively Irish peasants, but from a sense of devoir, and because 'tis expected from her and always had been expected of the Squire's Lady years without end. Cary and me were very Occupied making a Pot Pourri from a very good recipe she has. Tom presents my father with a new book of Post Roads, which he declares will be of great assistance to us in finding our way to Town. He has also had the goodness to hire 4 servants at Derby to accompany our Coach with pistols. The danger from Highwaymen is increasing every day now, and one hears nothing but of how Lady So and so was robbed on her way to town, and how Mr. This and That had a Blunderbuss held at his chest on Hounslow Heath, by a Gentleman of the Road.

Tom advises us to have by us a Purse containing Bad Money to deliver up if attacked, also a pistol each, with which to defend our Persons.

Cary and me had a Serious Talk together, and she gave me some very Excellent advice as to how to behave myself in Town. Amongst other things she warned me on no account to gamble for too high stakes, gossip of my Love affairs to my Female acquaintances, or permit a young gentleman to enter my room at night on any account whatsoever.

My father and Ned spending a very merry evening with Tom in the supper room, judging from the sounds which can be heard all over the house. Pray Heaven they do not drink too long or too deeply, for anything more Disagreeable than rumbling along in a Coach with a couple of cross Peevish men, still sleepy from a drinking bout can not be imagined. I myself must lay down my Pen and retire to bed for I am half dead.

## *May 19th*

Lord be praised ! in a few moments our Coach will have conveyed us away from this monstrously dull place. Mr.

and Mrs. Talbot, to whom brother Tom gave us letters
of recommendation, are as excellent a couple as one could
hope to see but hardly enlivening as Host and Hostess,
while as for their mansion house with its Greek porticos and
its monstrously great cold rooms, 'tis more fit to be a
Sepulchre than a human habitation. Last night Mrs. T.
read to us for 3 hours in the parlour from Milton's Paradise
Lost, regardless of the fact that we had travelled all day
over vile roads, till I dozed off and slipped from my chair.

To-night we lie at Squire Jodrell near Brixworth.

# NORTHAMPTON

*May 20th*

Here we are in a Filthy common Inn, brought here by a
prodigious mishap which occurred last evening. After a
tedious day over roads deep in Mud, we found ourselves
at nightfall by a kind of chalk pit, which at this part skirts
the high road. Heaven alone knows what happened,
whether a horse stumbled or a trace broke, but at all events
our Coach gave a mighty Heave, overturned and slipped
into the Pit, throwing Papa, Ned, Mrs. S. and self into a
Swearing Heap, and hurling Paddy and the Valets off the
box into Space. I swear I thought I was as good as Dead,
for the agitated horses began to kick the coach to bits; but
happily the mounted domestics flew to our rescue and
dragged us out from the Mêlé, bruised and mightily shaken,
but unscathed.

Mrs. S. Fell into Hysterics, Papa and Ned assisted to un-
loose the horses, while as for me, my only thought was to
rescue my wardrobe, which was scattered in all directions
over the ground. We were thankful to be alive and no
bones broken, but very put out at finding ourselves thus in
a lonely countryside with our chariot all in pieces and a
steady rain wetting us to the skin. We might have sat there
groaning all night, for there was not a sign of human
habitation, but to our Great relief after a time the Stage
coach most Providentially came into sight. We stopped the
coachman and finding that it was bound for London,
decided to take places for Papa, Ned, self and Mrs. S. and

a valet, leaving the other domestics to follow us later with the coach mended.

Ned at first Demurred somewhat at travelling in a Common stage, but my father silenced him, declaring that if he was so Proud he might sit in the rain all night and be damned to him, but he himself only wished to get to London and off the road as soon as possible. 'Twas then discovered that we had too much Baggage, for the Coach regulations only allow each passenger 14 lb. weight. This threw my father into a fury, but at length he agreed to relinquish the greater part of the baggage into Paddy's keeping. Then it seemed that there was only one place inside. I insisted on my father taking this on account of his Sciatica, while Ned, Mrs. S., and me climbed onto the roof. Ned in a Terrible Temper, but as for me I found my first ride on the stage coach highly diverting. We rattled along at such a Pace that I nearly fell off, having nothing but a small handle to keep myself steady. At the next stage a young naval officer clambered into the place next to me, and after gazing at me in the dusk with much curiosity said, "I'll swear, Ma'am, by your looks that your aren't accustomed to travel as an Outside." He said this with such a Quaint Naive Air that I burst out laughing, and seeing that he was a proper looking young man (indeed something about his Brown eyes and white teeth reminded me of Mr. A.), I answered that no, our chariot was smashed up and that I was an Irish lady on my Travels. We talked Amiably in this way for some time, then he put his cloak and arm round me to keep off the Rain, so he said, but so respectfully that I did not Demur. He told me some marvellous tales of his sea voyages, of Sea Serpents and Flying Fish, and how he had lived for months in the Indies as the lover of a savage Queen, but I cannot vouch for the truth of it all. I'll own I was vexed when a woman inside descended, and my father called me down to take her place. He was a killing devil. We arrived late at this place.

# III

# LONDON

*May 21st*

London at last, and I swear I am thankful for it too. We came all the way after our Mishap by stage coach, in spite of a heated argument between Papa and Ned, for the latter swore we ought to be Genteel and hire a Chaise, but my father declared that the stage would be safer and swifter, so we continued our journey in Flying Machines by leisurely stages. Our journey uneventful enough, for though the talk was of nothing but Highwaymen, not a sign of one did we see. Strange tales were told however, of highwaymen making their victims buy a dead Rabbit or something of that sort for an immense sum, and adventures were related by the passengers, some of which were too diverting to be True. The passengers all agreed that the presence of Gentry in the stage would attract Thiefs like Bees to a Honey Pot, and looked at us, which made us feel a trifle embarrassed. I was much diverted at the conversation of the passengers, and indeed they were the most varied collection imaginable, changing at every stage, red faced farmers, prim country ladies very apprehensive of being insulted, a young poet with Dirty Nails, a lawyer, and to our consternation at one moment, a lunatic in charge of a keeper, but he was made to sit by common consent on the Roof. Ned very disdainful and silent at all this, his nose in the air.

It seems that some stage coachmen are in League with these wicked Highwaymen.

Have completely forgotten, I see, a trifling adventure

last night at an inn at Finchley where we put up. I will own I did not care very much for the look of it, though the Landlady never ceased declaring that 'twas frequented by all the Quality, especially by the Irish gentry. We had a poor supper of eggs and bacon and retired to Dirty Beds. I was woken suddenly from my sleep by a monstrous loud clatter of shouting and thumping. My curiosity was roused, and I rushed to my door to see the cause of it all, half the Inn doing the same thing. Never saw a stranger scene. On the landing was a short ugly man in a shirt and top Boots, struggling with at least four others, while the Landlady stood by screaming. All this accompanied by Terrible Oaths and Yells; the short man being finally overpowered and carried downstairs kicking vigorously. A female in a dirty Nightcap had the complaisance to explain that the short man was a Highwayman who had been discovered in bed in the Inn, to the Vast alarm of everyone. I will own my first view of a Gentleman of the Road was very different from the Elegant masked figure I had imagined. My father mad at it all, and declared at first that he would remove baggage and all to a house of better repute, but we decided to remain where we were and retired again to bed. Have seen nothing of the Town as yet, for I am staying in till my Wardrobe arrives. This house in Hill Street very elegant.

## May 22nd

*"Carrots and Turnips Ho!"* This cry yelled in a Hoarse voice wakes me every morning. My father complains of the noise of London and indeed 'tis something Prodigious. The Watchmen are calling out the time and weather all night long, and when they have stopped the vendors of oranges, brooms, Matches, Rat Traps, Lord knows what else begin. For my part I find it very enlivening, but I am not surprised that the town ladies are as thin as Maypoles.

Am still much confused with this new house and the

many new domestics, whom I have put in Mrs. S.'s charge.
My father has bought me a very elegant Sedan chair with
4 bearers. It is to be at my disposition whenever I wish to
go out, and I intend to furnish it with rose satin cushions
and curtains. Seated in it and wearing my rose Brocade, I
flatter myself I shall be an Elegant sight.

Mrs. S. and me went out shopping this afternoon, for
though I expect my wardrobe by the carrier any day now,
I was careless enough to forget to bring a change of linen
with me on the stage, and my Chemise is now too dirty to
wear any longer. I purchased for myself several yards of
fine lawn at a Mercer's near here, and so I shall be decent
once more. The Damask here is 18s. a yard.

I am amazed at the vastness of this town and the Bustle
of coaches and Chairs in the streets. Never have I seen so
many pretty Women in so short a time. Pray Heaven Ned
will not lose his head. Our house is situated in the fashionable part of the town, and as far as I have been able to
observe to the East of us lies the trading and literary quarter
of the City, while to the West the town is ended at Hyde
Park. Mrs. S. tells me that Kensington Village is a very
modish spot where the Court ladies take country air.

### *May 23rd*

My first visitors to-day. Papa and Ned out at the cock pit
in Westminster to see a great battle between Sir John
Albury and Colonel Bellingham's black breasted reds. Was
reading Mrs. Scott's "Millennium Hall" in the afternoon in
the Salon, when I heard voices on the stairs. Was in deshabille thinking myself free from Intrusion, but thanks to
the swiftness of my Legs was able to run up to my room
and throw on my embroidered silk and arrange my hair a
trifle. Then descended and entered the room with an air
of Dignity, to find that my guests were no other than my
cousin, Lady Jane Atherton and her daughter Celia, both

wearing superb gowns, rouge and powder. 'Twas easy to
see they had come on purpose to examine me and see what
kind of a creature this Uncouth Irish relative was, for as I
entered they put up their quizzing glasses and stared at me
with open curiosity. With them was a young Gentleman,
whom they presented to me as Sir Miles Albury. Never
have I seen a droller sight than this pretty little Beau.
His clothes were embroidered stiff with gold and silver and
reeking with scent like a perfumers shop. He had the most
superb wig, shoes, amber cane, and snuff box that have ever
been seen, while as for his face, I dare swear one would
find Rouge and Powder on *his* Toilette table. I was so
amazed at the sight of him that I gazed open mouthed, and
it was evident by the way in which he Smiled and Smirked,
that he mistook my glance for one of admiration. To tell
the truth, I was thinking how Mr. A. would have Swal-
lowed him up, cane and all, in one gulp. Coz. Jane conversed very affably with me, but Cousin Celia who is
Blonde and very elegant, remained silent, fanning herself as
if about to faint, or when she spoke 'twas in a Mincing
voice, as if she had a bone stuck in her Throat. At last she
roused herself to say, "Is it true cousin, that you owe this
Grand Tour to a certain little intrigue with a handsome but
undesirable kinsman of yours? I have always heard that
your countrymen are immoderately handsome in a savage
way, but Lud stop me if I am becoming Indiscreet!" The
little beau laughed at this and said, " 'Pon my word,
Ma'am, I call it demmed wicked of you to twit your poor
cousin in this way. Why I declare you are making her
blush." This vexed me very much and I looked my mortification, I suppose, for my cousin seeing my discomfiture
went on, "Rumour has it," she said, "that he threatened
your father with a Blunderbuss, and tried to break into
your room and carry you off Bodily. Life must be monstrously diverting in Ireland what with Pigs and Murders
and Abductions!" At this I broke out Passionately that

Mr. Ancaster was a gentleman of very good parts and Breeding, who could write French and Latin and Italian as well as anyone. "Perhaps, Ma'am," I said Pertly, "you thing it uncivilised of a young man to be a good shot and horseman, and not strut about all day dressed up like a Peacock, and painted like a Woman," with a glance at Sir M. A. I regretted my sharp words a moment later, for I saw my cousins exchange a smile and I felt that doubtless I had made a fool of myself. In short I was thankful when they made their Adieux, soon after. Coz. J. invited me to a Rout at their house to which I replied with a Stiff Curtsey. I could see plainly enough that they did not admire either my Gown, my Person or my Manners. To tell the truth I regret now that I gave way to my Vexation. I believe too that 'twould have been more civil if I had offered them some refreshments, but I completely overlooked this in my Anger. Returned to my room very hot and ruffled at my first taste of London society, and was obliged to undo my gown and dip my face in cold water to restore my Calm.

### May 24th

To my great Amazement and joy Mrs. S. brought me a letter this morning from my dear Mr. A. The sly wretch has sent it under cover to her, and so we shall be able to correspond without my Father's knowledge. It commenced: "Dear Madam. Ever since your departure which robbed Co. Down of its fairest ornament, I have been debating in my mind whether or not I could have the boldness to send you this proof of my Constant and Undying love." I own I smiled somewhat at this unwonted timidity in my bold admirer. His letter went on to tell me how bitterly he regrets my absence, how life has lost all pleasure for him now, that he eats next to nothing and spends his whole time in melancholy rides past our house, or in translating

Homer's Odes by candlelight. "When you are all in the bustle of the beau monde," he wrote, "surrounded by admiring beaux, lost in a whirl of Routs, Plays, Balls and Card Parties, remember if only for a moment your disconsolate and lonely David. I assure you Ma'am, that I am getting quite wild and unkempt looking—a true Irish Bog-Dweller, now that your beautiful eyes are no longer there to examine and appraise my appearance.

"I study all night long, but Latin is a poor substitute for Love." The melancholy picture he drew of his condition, though I'll swear 'tis an imaginary one, filled my eyes with tears. I have written to assure him that I am continually thinking of him, and that contrary to his expectations I am already weary of London. When my letter will reach him Heaven only knows. 'Tis agitating to think what a distance lies between us. All to-day we have been receiving visitors, and the room at the foot of the stairs has been filled with footmen bringing most elegant notes to us, so it seems that our letters of recommendation will plunge us into a certain gaiety whether we will or no.

Among others Mr. and Mrs. D'Arcy came to pay their respects. They are near neighbours of Tom's. They brought their daughter with them, a slender tall Miss, very lovely with amiable and lustrous brown eyes. We conversed very pleasantly together. She is the agreeablest girl I have seen for some time. She was most elegantly attired in a gown of palest yellow, and has promised to take me to the best mercers in Town. She tells me she is near dead with gaiety, and this week has attended as much as seven parties a night. She also told me much diverting gossip. How that the King and Queen are unpopular, how all genteel Society is talking of the scandal caused by Lord Ilchester's daughter, Lady Susan Fox, having married an actor O'Brien, and how that not long ago two ladies of quality fought a duel

in the Park over the love of no less a person than the little
fop I met yesterday, though this last seems incredible!

Ned and me are to join their party at Ranelagh to-
morrow.

## *May 26th*

Yesterday Ned and me went to Ranelagh with Mrs.
D'Arcy, Miss D'Arcy and a merry party of half a dozen
elegant young gentlemen and ladies. I was much intrigued
at visiting this place I have heard such a prodigious lot of.
Indeed 'tis very fine with its great amphitheatre finely gilt,
painted and brilliantly illuminated. The entrance is but
12 pennies and so the place is frequented by every kind of
person and you can see cheek by jowl *filles de joie* and
ladies of fashion, country lawyers and beaux, in fact the
mob elbows the quality and 'tis all very lively and informal,
though not so dégagé as Vauxhall so I am told. We supped
to music. Ned very much catched by Miss D'Arcy, but she
has a preoccupied air about her and did not respond to his
attentions. Later Lord Suffolk and Miss Trevor Hamilton,
who are to be married this month, joined our table. A tall
melancholy young man by name of Mr. Sutcliffe was in
our party and appeared to admire my person—to judge by
the glances he cast in my direction. We did not exchange
a word till later in the evening when we strolled together
in the grounds, admiring the illuminations which were
Ravishing. We detached ourselves from the rest to speak
to Lady Aylesbury. Hearing that I was shortly setting out
for France, Mr. S. promised to lend me an interesting book
on the manners and customs of that country. When we
joined the party once more we found Miss D'Arcy very
pale, Ned, his arm in hers, evidently much pleased with
himself. Miss D'Arcy whispered to me that a party of
drunken young fellows had spoke to her, one having the
Insolence to call out, "Look at this pretty little trollop

I've found." Ned it seems played the Gallant Uomo and rescued her from their clutches. Poor Ned, if he could marry a charming girl like this, 'twould do him all the good in the world. At the moment he is too provokingly Complaisant.

Arrived back in Town at a very late hour, and hastened home in my chair with no less than four footmen carrying torches. Robberies are frequent even in this genteel part of the town. I received a letter from Cary to-day asking me to buy some Damask and Satin for her and to send her a good pattern for a cloak. She tells me to get these from the Mercers at the Hen and Chicken. For these purchases she sends me a Bank bill or rather the half of one. The other half is to come later, and this trick will secure the money against thieving post boys. I mean to send her a pretty fan as a present. To-night, we go to a card party at Lady Drogheda.

## May 27th

To Church. Wore my rose quilted gown.

## May 28th

Am in a mighty Bustle. Item bought to-day, 1 pair of dove silk shoes worked with silver thread, 1 pr. mouse coloured silk shoes for everyday, 5 yards of Mauve Satin for cloak and hood and what is over I shall get Mrs. Stewart to make into a cap. Am undecided over a coach for headdress or whether merely to wear flowers. The former is hideous in my opinion but all the rage. Must have my gown made lower in the Bodice. If one is blessed with a white bosom why conceal it? Apropos of clothes, Ned is attiring himself like a Lily of the Field. Has as many as 12 long waistcoats and all his shoes set with gold buckles. Lost £10 at Loo at My Lady Drogheda.

### *May 29th*

To the play in Lady Mary Coke's box. I blushed so at some parts I scarce knew which way to look. The actors pelted with apples and oranges.

### *June 1st*

Rout at Coz. Atherton. Wore plum brocade, Sumptuous. Lord M——rd is a handsome creature but he thinks all London is his Seraglio. I shall be happy to show him his error.

### *June 2nd*

Vauxhall. Down the river with Lord M.'s party. All very merry. Ned and Lord M——rd a trifle too much so.

### *June 4th*

Cary safely delivered of a son. Thank Heaven for this. Papa in Raptures.

### *June 6th*

All the Town is laughing at the escapade of the Duke. The Wild young man exercised his shooting across Hanover Square and near killed poor old General Denbigh in the opposite house. They say the bullet whistled past his ear and lodged in the wainscotting. Ned returned utterly drunk last night from the Maccaroni Club. They are travelled Young Men who do great Execution with Spy glasses. He is very gay of late. Lost £15 at Whisk. 'Tis cards all day and night long, and 'tis Ill bred to refuse to play. I play like a Fool and am losing Heavily.

### June 7th

Miss D'Arcy sick. Pray heaven 'tis not the Smallpox. She will not permit me to visit her for fear it is, but I sent her flowers and also a Sweet embroidered purse to comfort her. Ned very unhappy to hear of her Indisposition.

Last night Ned and me went to an Assembly at Madame Cornelys at Carlisle House in Soho Square. Magnificent rooms and collation and a Crush that near killed me. Lord M——rd very attentive to me.

### June 8th

Miss D'Arcy recovered somewhat. Not the dread sickness. I spend all my Days now at Routs or at Mrs. Dantin, Mount Street. Am growing thin.

### June 10th

Saw King and Queen out driving to-day. Not an Immoderately lovely couple, but I huzzahed and waved my handkerchief with the best of them. Burletta last evening at Convent Garden. Laughed till I near Split.

It seems there is a Plan on foot that Ned should be painted by Mr. Reynolds who is the Painter à la Mode now. I declare I cannot see why Ned with his Carroty Locks should have his portrait made while my more worthy Features should go down unrecorded to the Tomb. Have prayed Papa to permit me to be painted by Miss Reid who is also very Modish but he declares he has not sufficient money for two, which I vow is a Monstrous shame.

### June 11th

Haymaking party. Amongst Guests: Lord M., Mr. Sutcliffe, Lord Tavistock and his pretty betrothed, Lady E.

Keppell, Madame de Guerchey, Lady Mary Duncan and so on. Lord M——rd very attentive to La Belle Irlandaise as he pleases to call me. Unluckily the weather broke and the rain spoiled our Sweet Bucolic Simplicity, soaking Pet Lambs, Muslin Frocks, and making us into a mob of drowned Rats.

### June 13th

Mr. Sutcliffe visits me nearly every morning at my toilette with books. Sits and glares like an idiot. Lost another £30 at Piquet the other day. My father's face will be grim when I inform him of this.

### June 15th

Lady H. is the greatest Rake in Town. Her minauderies are Intolerable.

### June 16th

Breakfast with Lady Temple. All the polite World present. Coffee, chocolate, biscuits, cream, buttered toasts, tea and Scandal. Mr. Sutcliffe took me to Bathoe in the Strand for Italian books. Pointed out to me Chevalier d'Eon, a strange looking Wretch. They tell the most curious tales of him. Some swear he is really a Female in disguise.

### June 18th

I spend half the day at the Hairdresser's now. My head has not been opened for over a Fortnight, and this is positively the longest time I will go in this hot weather, though some Ladies keep their Heads unopened till they are Intolerable to themselves and everyone else. The dresser informed me that one lady from motives of thrift went so long a time that her head when opened was found to contain a Nest of Mice. Lord save me from that! We are to attend a grand Ball to-night at the Duchess of Queensbury. She is a Whimsical clever woman.

## June 19th

Philosophical lecture with Mr. Sutcliffe. Somewhat wearisome. Have hopes of seeing Lord M——rd at the Little Theatre to-night.

## June 20th

Was mightily distressed this morning. Out shopping perceived a Poor youth being conducted to execution for Highway robbery. He could not have been more than 18 with an Amiable, handsome countenance and an air of Breeding. What a Melancholy end for a foolhardly escapade. Mr. Sutcliffe thinks they hang for too Trifling Offences. If I was Queen of England I should change this, but most persons I talk to are all for Hanging everyone.

## June 21st

Attended a Magnificent Masque last night at Northumberland House, which did not cease till 7 in the morning.

I dressed as a Turkish slave in a rich costume of Silver cloth. 'Twas a Splendid sight. All the Beauties of the Town as Cleopatras, Goddesses, Shepherdesses and so on. One gentleman attired as a dead Corpse in a Shroud and carrying a Coffin. So Ghastly a spectacle that one lady swooned at the sight of him. Saw the famous, or some would say, infamous Miss Chudleigh in some sort of Undress. To my mind she is somewhat decayed. They say she is married to Mr. Hervey of the Navy. Supper and lighting on a grand scale. Ned declares there must have been no less than a 100 dishes. I believe he tasted of them all. One's head confused with it all. Duchess of Rutland to my mind is marvellously handsome.

Lord M——rd prodigiously magnificent as a Turkish Sultan (could anything be more apropos?). Danced many times with me and said glancing at my costume, "I must find a Sultana for myself, Ma'am," which Fluttered me a trifle. Wish I knew his meaning. Also complimented me on the length of my eye lashes.

*June 23rd*

An odious and utterly Unexpected Mishap occurred to me last night! Was returning with Lady D. from the play in her coach. 'Twas a dark raining night. As we passed through St. James' Square our horses stopped suddenly, there was a noise of scuffling and shouts, the window was pulled open, and a Masked Ruffian thrust his head in and presented a pistol at our breasts with the words, "Damee stand and deliver—off with those jewels now." Words cannot depict our Fright and Consternation. Lady D. in her anger swore like a Trooper and I very rashly attempted to jump out of the coach and call for the Watchman. A pistol held against my very bosom made me realise the hopeless position we were placed in. Weeping with Rage and Vexation I removed my Jewels, while Lady D. did likewise. The Villain then galloped away. I lay the night at Lady D.'s house being too agitated to return home and we spent half the night in Fruitless Lamentations. I have lost by this Dastardly Outrage the following ornaments—my diamond earrings left me by Great Aunt Caroline, my diamond and ruby chain and pendant given me by my dear Mama on her very death bed, a curious and antique pearl ring, two diamond rings, a bracelet set in brilliants and my jewelled fan. 'Tis Monstrous and Damnable that such a

Thing should happen in London. Travelling in the country one may be prepared for Robbery, but Town should at all events be safe. The Watchmen are worse than useless. 'Tis Abominable. Lady D. and my father have offered large rewards to the Bow Street Runners, but they are Fools too and I dare swear we shall never see one of those trinkets again. Am too Vexed to go abroad to-day. Have received many amiable messages from my friends condoling me.

*June 25th*

Supper party last night given in my honour by Lord M. to console me, so he declared, for my recent highway robbery. A large Company present. All extremely Lively. Lord M. no eyes for anyone but me. He wrote my name on his wine glass with a diamond and then to my vast confusion pulled off my red satin slipper, filled it with wine, and drank my Health from it. This extravagance agitated me and seeing that most of the company were intoxicated, I pulled Ned to one side and made him escort me home.

This morning received a note from Lord M. as follows. "Lord M——rd's Compliments to Miss Knox. Hopes she was not Offended last night? What was the reason for her sudden departure which robbed the Party of its Chief Grace? He begs her to send him one of her Chemises, for he has vowed not to drink another drop of Wine that has not been strained through a Piece of her Underlinen."

This strange message somewhat Disconcerted me. For some time could not decide whether he was really madly Enamoured or merely insulting me. At length I decided that a bantering reply would be the most discreet under the circumstances, and I sent a line to the effect that Irish Lawn was too precious by far to be used as a Seive.

Miss D'Arcy to take tea to-day. She made me laugh heartily by showing to me a letter from a young Gentleman in the Army, who, being on Guard, responded to her invitation in this strange manner, "Captain Pole regrets he cannot accept Kind Invitation, but is Prematurely confined in the Tower"!

*June 27th*

Ranelagh. Lord M——rd came up to me as meek as a Lamb and full of apologies. Wish to Heaven he would declare himself one way or another.

Very Gay Party with Lady T. She is the most Vivacious woman imaginable. Said to-day apropos of the new Gentry, "Lud! I dare not spit out of the window now for fear of spitting on an Earl," which made us all scream. The story going the rounds is that the Duke of G. attempting to appease his mistress, Dolly Carsons, with whom he had had a Tiff, gave her a Bank Bill for £100, whereupon she cried, "Damn your money, what's the use of it," clapped it between two bits of Bread and eat it. I wish someone would offer it to me for I am in Debt to a Shocking Extent, and dare not inform Papa. I would borrow from Ned but he, it would seem, is still more Embarrassed. 'Tis all these Odious Cards that are to blame. I console myself by thinking that I could be in a Worse Case. I have seen a lady lose as much at £700 at a game.

The town is growing Empty now.

*June 30th*

Have been sick these last few days of l'influenza, a Fashionable Sickness for many of my friends are suffering from it, but it has ended my Gaieties for a while.

My father ordered me to be bled, but I locked my door and lay abed silent though my father and the Surgeon battered on my door in a Fury. Thanks to Mrs. S.'s gruels am now quite recovered though as weak as a Mouse.

## July 2nd

To-day taking the air in my chair, one of my Bearers fell in a hole in the road and all but threw me out on to the street. Saw the famous Gunning, Duchess of Hamilton, out. What a Fortune she and sister gained by their looks. No sign from Lord M. d——n him.

## July 3rd

Went to a Drum at Lady Waldgrave and heard all the Scandal I had missed by my Sickness. It seems that Lord P. wedded Lady E. H. chiefly to escape from 2 importunate mistresses. Another Droll tale is that poor Mr. Astor fell enamoured of Miss Johnson, daughter to a Poor country Squire, for her beautiful brown Locks. The morning after they were wed, lo and behold! the slut threw her "tête" aside, displaying Carroty hair which colour Mr. Astor holds in particular Abhorrence.

Out to-day saw a Press gang seize upon 2 young men. Thought for a brief second there would be a Riot among the Mob to rescue them.

## July 5th

Guests including Mr. Sutcliffe to dinner at 3. Stayed till 8 exchanging Gossip and Compliments. Purchased some new caps and corsets for myself. Miss D'Arcy has given me an excellent Recipe for Lip Salve. Ned is abroad all night now with parties of wild blades, and seems to indulge in every kind of Rakery and Frolic from his account.

Last night, so it seems, at some tavern his friends threw the table and chairs out of window, and on the landlady remonstrating threw her after her chattels. Someone less drunk than the rest called out that she might be dead, whereupon some Tipsy Wit cried out, "Charge her in the bill." Happily for her and them the window was near the ground, and the poor woman was still alive and unhurt. I told Ned somewhat severely that these Excesses will lead him to Tyburn in a country where one is hanged for cutting down an Apple Tree. I added sharply that insulting women and knocking down feeble old watchmen was a poor kind of wit in my opinion, and upon this we had a Furious Quarrel which raged till my father ordered me to my room and Ned to leave the house.

### July 6th

Have made a most Astounding discovery to-day. Miss D'Arcy came to take tea with me and after sitting for some time in Deep Dejection suddenly broke out: "My dear friend, I must confide in you. I am in a most odious predicament. In short I am well—'enceinte.'" "What," I cried, "my Poor Child, have you been so foolish as to allow yourself to be . . ." "No, not at all," said she, a trifle offended and pulling out from her dress a Chain she is accustomed to wear round her neck, showed me a Wedding Ring attached to it. "Married," I cried, much relieved, "not that I would have set myself up to judge you for I as near as near did the other thing myself once." Anyhow, the whole story came out, how that she had made the acquaintance while visiting friends in Shropshire, of a young naval officer of Poor but Genteel parentage. They had become mutually Enamoured, and knowing that her Parents would never permit them to wed, they had the ceremony performed in secrecy.

He is on service now and she, poor Lady, in the condition she confessed to me. We sat for over 3 hours discussing her Predicament, but after consuming a vast quantity of Tea and Cakes were still monstrously undecided. At length I counselled her to confess the whole affair to her parents, or if her Courage failed her, I myself was willing to break the news to them.

She departed somewhat Fortified, and is to inform me to-morrow of her Decision.

Who would ever have suspected such a thing? I own I Quail somewhat at the prospect of informing Mr. D'Arcy of his Daughter's Indiscretion. I tremble to think of Ned's vexation when he hears of it, for I truly believe he is catched by her.

*July 7th*

Here I am locked up in my chamber, my eyes so swollen with crying that I can scarcely see out of them. I believe to day has been the most Terrible of my life. Misfortunes appear to be overwhelming me. Early this morning I received a distracted letter from poor Lydia D'Arcy bidding me an Eternal Farewell. She has confessed all, and her parents are dispatching her away post haste to an Aunt, Lady Montgomery, in the wilds of Devonshire to repent at leisure. I wept somewhat at perusing this and wondered if I should ever set eyes on my poor Friend again. Then to add to my misery, that fool Mr. Sutcliffe, took it into his Head to wait on my father and ask for my Hand. My father summoned me to the parlour when he had left, and informed me of his offer adding that he hoped I would accept it, as Mr. Sutcliffe was an "excellent young man"; these were his very words, and the owner of a good property in Sussex. I regret to say that I flew into a Pretty Passion at this, declaring that I would as soon wed a Mute as that long-visaged, melancholy Idiot and that I wished to Heaven my father would leave me in Peace. While we were wrangling in this manner, he roaring at me and I commencing to Weep, in came Ned and had the Impudence to give his opinion on the matter, saying that I was a Damned fool not to take a good offer like that, and still more of a Fool to hang around hoping for that Rake Lord M——rd to declare himself! This remark provoked me so terribly that I turned on him exclaiming: "Well, sir, let me tell you that Miss D'Arcy is a married Woman"; whereupon Ned's curses were so terrible that I was forced to clap my hands over my ears.

My father in a fury drove us out of the room, and me up to my chamber. Later he came to me, and declared that I had grown alarmingly Passionate and Ill humoured of late since my stay in Town, and he could not think what had come over me.

"Now girl," he said, "have some sense and take Mr. S."

At this I stamped my foot and said: "I will never wed anyone but Mr. Ancaster, and these are my last words on the subject."

"Very well," roared my father, "very well. You shall stay up here till your temper has abated," and slammed the door to, adding as he went out, "What you require, Miss, is a good bleeding."

'Tis true enough I have been in a Vile Mood this last week or so. I believe it is the Heat. Heaven, or rather my father, knows how long I shall be confined up here.

*July 8th*

Nothing to write for I am still cruelly confined to this room. The servants dare not release me, for Papa is as Absolute as the King of France.

*July 9th*

A fresh calamity has occurred. Ned contrived to slip into my room looking very flustered, when the Footman brought me my dinner. Fell upon me with the words: "My dear Cleone, I am in a damnable scrape." In short, Ned, like the Idiot he is, has picked a quarrel with a Young

Gentleman of Importance (no less a person than a cousin of Mr. Pitt's) who has challenged him to a Duel. I am, by some means or other to induce my father to depart prematurely for Bath, while Ned remains behind on pretence of staying with Mr. Richards at his villa at Knightsbridge. Gracious Heaven, this is an odious business! If he slays his opponent I should not be astonished if he was obliged to fly the country. I cannot think why these hateful calamities have occurred all in a Heap. No more now.

# IV

# BATH

*July 12th*

I write this at Woolhampton at the Rising Sun Inn. A moderately easy journey. Passed securely through Hounslow Heath and Maidenhead Thicket unmolested by Road Inspectors. Most unhappily however poor Paddy has utterly disgraced himself, and my father has been constrained to dismiss from our service this Faithful and hitherto Trusty Retainer. A most unlooked for Misfortune. Occurred in this manner. To-day, a little way past Reading, the Stage Coach came up at a Swift Pace and outstripped our Chariot, the coachman meanwhile jeering at our domestics. Paddy, mortified, whipped on the horses, the Stage quickened up and so we raced neck to neck, careering round corners at a terrible Pace and rocking from Side to Side. Papa cursed, the passengers screamed, Mrs. S. and self were Thrown violently in a Heap. Thank the Lord our hind wheel stuck in a rut, and only this I am convinced, saved us from overturning. The Stage speedily outdistanced us. Papa, mad with Rage, damned Paddy in a Frightful Manner. The poor Wretch unable to give any reason for this Wicked Mad conduct but, maintained with tears in his eyes his passionate desire to Vindicate the Family Honour in the eyes of the Stage. Am sure 'twas nothing but an unpremeditated Impulse on the part of the poor Rash Wretch, but Papa declares we could never trust him now on the Continent. This Inn is more like a country residence, for Lord S——n is lying here, and has in his customary domineering fashion made the place His Own even to putting the Domestics in his livery.

## July 13th

This place is filled with gouty old noblemen and their ladies, statesmen, poets, writers, admirals, beauties, Beaux and fortune hunters. All meet in the Pump Room, drink water and exchange Gossip. Thankful I have my elegant Town Wardrobe. Do not know if I shall care for this place, but am vastly happy to be away from Town, where my last days were rendered Odious by Papa, the heat and Lord M. My father treats me with great solicitude, the result of my fit of Vapours in Town, but Lud! I tremble to think of his wrath if he could but know what Ned was up to! I shall not be easy in my mind till this hateful Rencontre is safely finished with. Though Ned has often Plagued me in the Past, I pray Highest Heaven he will not be run through. My father escorted me to the chief physician here, and remained closeted with him some time, doubtless demanding him what Malady is the cause of my Infatuation for Mr. A. and my recent Wilfulness. At all events, the pompous Medico after examining my tongue and gazing down my throat, prescribed for me a course of Medicinal waters adding: "Res est soliciti plena timori amor. Vitiant artus —— contagia mentis." To which my father replied: "Varium et mutabile semper Faemina." And they both laughed to my vexation. Papa informs me that this Latin stands for: "Love is the perpetual source of fear and anxiety. When the mind is ill at ease, the body is in a certain degree affected," and also: "Woman is always changeable and capricious," which shows plainly what fools men are.

## July 14th

This is a beautiful place, set in an amphitheatre of

rocky and wooded hills, and has spacious and elegant houses and a fine Abbey Church, but for my part I am already a trifle weary of it, though heaven knows 'tis crowded enough with the Beau Monde. I have met several of my London acquaintances, but 'tis nothing but Complaints of Vapours and Gout, Stale Scandal dished up from the past season and spiteful cries of, "Heavens, look at her face." "Lud! how plain she is grown," and so on. No news from Ned.

### *July 15th*

To church. A sermon so lengthy that I near died. Dozed behind my fan.

### *July 16th*

To the Baths for the first and last time, that's flat! Clad in a Bonnet, Jacket and Petticoat (a costume that does not become me) the Ladies here contrive to conduct watery flirtations and Intrigues as happily as on Terra Firma. Each lady is provided with a little Tray ladened with sweetmeats and perfumes, and when these float away out of reach the gentlemen swim after them gallantly, to the Admiration of the Spectators in the gallery.

Miss Ralston in particular was as Frolicsome as a Mermaid and displayed a very fine pair of arms. For my part I feel too Healthy now I am out of Town, to enjoy being conveyed in a chair swathed in blankets as if I was a gouty old Dame, and I have no "beau" with whom to disport myself in the water. Apropos of these Baths, Miss R. tells me a diverting little "conte", how that last season a Dowager Marchioness of excessively Tall stature and overweening pride ordered the Bath to be filled to her chin, whereupon all the Ladies of lower rank and height were obliged to hasten out or be drowned!

## July 17th

Time passes here in the same insipid, gay manner every day. Morning in Undress at private or public breakfasts, drinking waters, baths; evening prayers at the Abbey for the Devout, social parades, visits to the Libraries and book-sellers, the Eternal Cards. After dinner more parades, tea, drives and perhaps a Ball at the Assembly Rooms. I wish Ned were here, for he would Enjoy the Cricket which all the young gentlemen here indulge in. Old gentlemen abound here, and are never Weary of informing one how marvellously Refined and Decorous the Society was in the Golden Days of Beau Nash, "before, ma'am, all these Damned tradesmen and negro drivers made it all so common." The young gentlemen write verses, little tortured vers d'esprits to their Belles, and they are entered in a book at the booksellers. I have had 3 addressed to me, but they are Too Insipid and Weak to waste time and Paper upon copying them in. I suspect that they find my name not an easy one for rhyming, else one poor Youth would not have been constrained to couple Cleone with *Moaning!*

## July 18th

Lord G.—— has arrived here with a Blackamoor and 3 kept mistresses in his retinue. What Lady G. thinks of this Seraglio is not reported. She retires to the Wells for her Bathing and doubtless consoles herself. Apropos of Negros, I saw the following notice in the newspaper here: "Black Boy for sale, Docile and obedient. Answers to the name of Toby," which so catched me that I wished to answer it, but my father sternly forbid me to add to our Retinue which already it seems, is costly enough. He makes great Complaints of our expenditure in Town and forbids me to purchase any more Wardrobe for some little time.

I walk here everyday in the Meadows and by the River Avon. Papa and I ride together.

### *July 19th*

Am vexed to-day. No sound from Ned. Heaven help the poor Foolish Youth. Also Miss R. in conversation on various people mentioned Lord M——rd, and declared that he was Loved by half the women of Fashion in Town, but that he would never be dragged to the Altar by anyone of them in her opinion, for he had several mistresses, and though many beautiful young Ladies had striven to capture him, some even being Complaisant beyond the bounds of Virtue and Prudence in an attempt to compromise him, he had each time eluded their grasp. It seems that when they weep and lay the blame for their ruin on him, he replies with the utmost callousness: "Dear Madam, why distress yourself? There is always the Foundling Hospital." I think now with Deep Mortification of certain Vain Foolish hopes which I once cherished. Is it likely that a man who can have half the Beauties of London as his concubines would deign to offer poor me the coveted Title of Sultana?

I shall pluck his now Hateful image from my heart, thankful that though humiliated I have at all events preserved my Good Name.

### *July 20th*

Fulfilled my promise to Mrs. Soames and examined Mrs. Winters' Seminary for Young Ladies here. I do not believe Elizabeth Soames would thrive in such a place. Mrs. W. makes a monstrous to do about her instruction which if one is to believe her, comprises Latin, Greek, Hebrew, French, Italian, Dancing, Music, Keeping Accompts, Arithmetic, Singing, History, Pastry Cooking,

Lud! I have forgot what else, but I observed that the Pupils were Dirty and Ill kempt and I doubt if they are taught Grace of Carriage by their general Deportment. I should not be astonished also if they were kept short of Food.

A new married couple, Mr. and Mrs. Chetwyn, arrived here on their Wedding trip accompanied by Mrs. Peel their Aunt. They are excessively young, 17 and 18 respectively, and were wedded by Force to cancel a Gambling Debt between their Parents, but seem vastly happy notwithstanding.

*July 21st*

A play acted in a Barn near here by the fashionable youth of the place, in which I played the role of "Clarissa", a young country lady who is betrayed by a noble Rake. Thankful that though the Bucolic character of the part fits me, the other does not through some Happy Chance, for I own to my shame that I have not always shewn sufficient prudence, especially where Mr. David Ancaster was concerned; so Fatal an effect does swarthy masculine beauty produce upon my too susceptible Heart.

The play was poorly acted as might have been anticipated from the rehearsals, where all the players wrangled and complained of their Roles. "My dear, I vow I cannot be an Ingenue! 'Tis too Insipid! Let me be the fascinating Lady Georgina! I am immoderately skilful at passionate scenes," and so on. My Noble Rake, far from being the Bold Villain he was pictured in the play, was seized all on a sudden with a fit of fright and totally forgot his words till I pinched his arm sharply, whereupon he bleated: "Clarissa, I am determined to have you Body and Soul" in a voice like a sheep! Before 'twas ended it commenced to rain and the Barn being Old and Decayed, the spectators retired home damp and melancholy.

*July 23rd*

Ned arrived by post chaise, excessively pallid, arm in sling. Mr. P. wounded in Lungs and is hovering between life and death. Decided after consultation that the sooner we reach France the better, lest the worst should happen. Juries, owing to Mr. P.'s influential position would in all certainty pass a severe verdict. Pray Heaven we can persuade my father to move. No more now, for there is much to be done. To convey at such short notice an Obstinate Father, family coach, 5 domestics and impedimenta is no easy Task. Papa at my Ernest intercession has pardoned Paddy, but Mrs. S. to my vast amazement, has utterly refused to brave yet another sea voyage, which is damnably odious of her. She is to remain here with Lady Brownlow and I shall hire a Frenchwoman to take her part. Papa very Vexed at this.

## V

## FRANCE

*July 28th—Amiens*

My father's ill opinion of the French fully confirmed, for on arriving here, we discovered that the Innkeeper at Calais had pilfered our boxes and stolen a quantity of linen ruffles and a gilt snuff box. On the other hand 'tis not Impossible that they were purloined on board the Pacquet Boat, for we were all as uneasy as anything after 8 hours passage, and not caring for anything except to be set on shore once more.

Ned and me much Diverted to find ourselves in this strange Country, and I hung my head out of the coach window all the journey down to this place admiring the sights, but my father complains greatly of the rain which he never observes in his native land, but which vexes him here; the French louis for which he reluctantly parts with his precious Sterling, and the Rapacity of the people in general.

A great quantity of English pass this route, and we are expected to path our way with gold. Ned had a sharp Dispute with the Customs apropos of a new Green Plush coat. He speaks the language admirably, to my astonishment.

The country round here is poor and but indifferently pretty, but the roads are superb. Inns bad, with poor wine and bread, but I am delighted at the newness of it all, the Poplars, clothes of French peasants, unaccustomed Tongue, and we have occasional glimpses of fine Chateaux. I am vain enough to be Diverted with the Attention and

74

Curiosity our appearance excites. This Town seems prosperous. A cavalary regiment quartered here. Two very genteel young officers escorted us around the Gothic Cathedral which we visited to-day, explaining all the Beauties of it to us. Was gratified to note that I can converse very Tolerably in French. Believe I shall be happy in this Country; if Mr. A. were but here.

### July 29th

Travellers see Curious sights indeed. Last evening 2 young gentlemen arrived at our Auberge in a chaise. Both elegantly attired, one smaller and younger than the other. To all appearances Brothers. I observed that the younger brother seemed vexed when the tall young man cast a casual sheep's eye in my direction, but thought no more of it. This morning coming downstairs I passed their chamber and glanced in, the door being ajar. What was my surprise to perceive seated on the bed in Deshabille not 2 young men, but One young man and a Pretty girl with long black hair. Yet two young Gentlemen left the Inn half an hour later.

Indeed, this is a strange country where such Miracles occur! Who the young Friends were no one can tell me, nor is it my business to know, but it has given me an idea for my next Masquerade. I vow I should look monstrous fine in Breeches and a Tie Wig.

### August 6th—Chanteloup

Never have I seen or indeed dreamed of any place so magnificent as this. 'Tis truly more a palace than a mere dwelling place. The rooms are large, spacious, and furnished in the heights of Elegance and Taste, many hung with exquisite Tapestry. My own room is the prettiest I have seen for some time, with a charming gilded bed hung with Rose satin, Toilette tables and chairs en suite. The walls are hung with rare tapestry depicting the Life of Venus. Everywhere one glances are fine gilt mirrors, clocks and vases of priceless value. 'Tis fit for a Princess, for every article in the room is an objet de luxe. Down below all equally fine. The style is excessively Formal, but in keeping, in my opinion, with the place. Attached to the house is an Immense Pleasure ground which I have not yet had leisure to observe carefully, but it supplies this Mansion with a Thicket of sweet scented and rare Flowers and Fruit. Have been so utterly bewildered by all the Sumptuousness that I have not dared approach my journal. My poor pen is not equal to the Task of describing it. The Duchesse treats us with the greatest Amiability and shows us every Egards. She is Charming and Petite. The weather has become so Excessively Hot that we are mightily thankful to reserve our stay in Paris till later. The guests here are numerous, everything being on a gigantic scale, and I have not yet been able to ascertain their names and titles as yet, but all belong to the Haute Noblesse. Among others the Duc de Nivesnoir, Duchesse de Cosse and Duchesse de La Valliere who is excessively handsome, though over 50 years of age. The Va et Vient however is Prodigious and new Guests arrive every Hour. A great Bustle and Buz if ever there was one. The Ladies here wear Immense Heels. Their Heads smaller than in England, but excessively Fuzzed. They are Witty and Elegant, but do not possess to my mind the fine forms and complexions of English-women. Indeed 'tis hard to say what kind of faces they have, for they are all Rouged and Painted to an Immoderate degree. What they think of my Appearance and Hair 'tis hard to say. I believe they consider my foreign dress and speech piquant, at all events they treat me with great courtesy. One lady informed me indeed that the french prefer the Irish to the English, who according to her account have Uncouth Manners when travelling on the

Continent, and will even appear in genteel french society
in Hunting Suits, which causes Vast Scandal. I am Vastly
Surprised at the Tone in general of the Conversation which
is utterly different from what I had thought 'twould be.
Had expected Frivolity, but the talk here among both
sexes is of nothing but Politics, Literature and Religion.
I own I am somewhat melancholy at finding this Grave
Air. The Gentlemen are stiff and Philosophical. The Ladies
are all Savante or pretend to be. I am not prepared to
swear that they do not indulge in Affairs de Coeur, and
that the men are not Fond and the ladies frail like plain
mortals, but at all events they have a very curious manner
of conducting their Intrigues. I think Mr. A. would be
very Melancholy here.

For the rest our mode of life is sumptuous and we pass
our days in Elegant Leisure. The morning as we please.
Dinner at 3 or 15 o'clock as 'tis called quaintly in France.
Cards and conversaton with our Hostess, bed when we
choose, in short, all Very dégagé except for Supper when
we dress as Magnificently as if at Versaille. No Demands
of "When are you going?" or "Why don't you do this or
t'other?" We live like Gods and Goddesses upon Olympia.
The domestics comprise a small Army. Ned declares there
must be no less than 400, indoor and outside. My father
lost in admiration of the Pigeries and Poultry Yards.

### August 7th

A letter from my dear Cary. It seems that William is the
lustiest Babe for his age, that ever was seen in Derbyshire.
Sir C. Mills is to wed a Widow.

### August 10th

A play acted most admirably in the private theatre here.
Even the performances of the most noted English actors

would seem Insipid to me besides this Vivacious and Witty Miming. Their very hands seemed to speak. I own I find the french more entertaining on than off the stage. The talk now is of nothing but Religion or rather Abuse of it. 'Tis the Mode to be an Atheist and a Heathen. Monsieur de Belisle a relative and protégé of the Duchess, expressed Prodigious Contempt when I confessed that I was a Devout Protestant. "Fancy, Mademoiselle is a dévote" he announced sneeringly to the Company and there was a general titter. I was Revenged notwithstanding this, for later he mentioned Richardson's "Clarissa Harlowe" in terms of highest praise, whereupon 'twas for me to cry out that the Novelist was utterly Demodé now in England. The young man in Question is short and has no chin and besides, all this Philosophy in my opinion does not add to the attraction of a young gentleman. How different indeed from my ardent Mr. A. Pray Heaven I shall find a letter from him in Paris. My father declares that he observes a vast alteration in french manners since he visited this country as a young man. Then, the Petits Maitres talked and thought of nothing but Gallantry. He is prepared to wager that these Intellectual Airs are but a superficial covering for the National Licentiousness.

*August 11th*

Out riding to-day in the forest with a party of ladies and gentlemen. Monsieur de Belisle, perhaps thinking that my figure looked well in a riding suit, attached himself to me and attempted to convert me to Atheism. But I laughed in his face and rode ahead so fast that he could not keep up with me. My horsemanship much praised to Papa by the company. The forest here is magnificent with broad roads cut in it. It is well stocked with deer and boars. Returning home by the high road we passed by a village. Was astonished by the dirtiness and general aspect of poverty. The cottages were hovels, peasants unkempt and some barely clothed. More like parts of Ireland, but my father declared he would be ashamed to see *his* tenants in Co. Down in such a filthy and disorderly state. It seems that the taxes are very heavy on the "tiers états," the nobles and clergy are free from this, which doubtless accounts for their great riches. I have a coverlid on my bed composed entirely of Venice point, my sheets trimmed with the finest lace. Thank Heaven, I have a lovely wrapper and cap of rose satin, or I should not dare to lie in all this splendour.

*August 12th*

Some of the company here are excessively strange. Madame d'Harcourt who is lovely to a degree, is affectation itself. She never blows her nose for fear of spoiling its outline, but dabs at it with a piece of lawn which her page carries for her. She refuses also to eat anything in public except fruit and biscuits. This morning she informed me she cannot sleep except in a sitting position with flowers on her pillow, and other absurdities. She has had three husbands, all of whom she has driven to their graves, and heaven knows how many lovers, although she is not more than thirty five or so. Madame la Comtesse de Brinoy de Chateauroux on the other hand is a most elegant and charming lady. She must be more than sixty years, yet she has all the vivacity and fascination of a young woman. Her form is slim and supple, her skin soft and fresh as a child's. She possesses in short an elegant mind and body. She treats me with great amiability, and has given me some Valuable Advice with regard to Mr. A. and Men in General. This morning in the enclosed garden where I helped her gather herbs to make into a complexion wash she said "My dear Child, do you know how I have Retained my looks? All my life I have been loved and all my life I have eaten vegetables. Do the same and if you do not use too much rouge, you will keep your youth beyond the usual limit; in short, you will have a longer lease of life than the rest of your sex, for to be ugly is to be as good as dead." All this is very true.

## August 13th

Last night our hosts held a fête champêtre. A magnificent affair. The grounds all illuminated with torches and lanterns. A sumptuous supper served in the hall and in the garden. Sprightly music, and a troupe of Opera Dancers performing on the lawn. There was even a flock of lambs festooned with blue ribbons to give a bucolic air. The guests were all attired as Shepherds and Shepherdesses or Greek Gods and so on. Madame de Brinoy had the goodness to assist me with my costume. As Pomona, Nymph of Gardens, I wore a green gown ornamented with flowers, grapes in my hair and a silver pruning knife in one hand. Looked very passable indeed. A party of gypsies hired by the Duchesse to tell fortunes in the Rose Garden. One swarthy hag seized my hand and poured out a stream of prophecy. Among a great deal of foolishness one remark of hers seems to me worthy of note. She declared that my fate was a handsome dark young man who loved me passionately, that there were difficulties in our path, but that if I wished for happiness, I must remain faithful to him. This without any doubt points most clearly to Mr. A. She then declared that Happiness would come to me on the water, and incomprehensible though this is to me, I heartily pray it may be true.

Happened during the Fête to observe an incident which caused me some surprise. Was near the wood to look for a fan I had dropped, when a Bacchante ran lightly across the grass. She looked round and made a sign. Whereupon she was joined by a gentleman dressed as a Satyr and they hurried hand in hand into the thicket. I meanwhile being hidded in the shadow of a tree, perceived by the light of the moon that the couple were Madame d'Harcourt and Monsieur de Damville.

Turning to go I perceived at my elbow no less a person than Madame de Damville—a captivating blonde. She was smiling very quizzingly behind her mask and pointing in their direction with her fan, she observed in the coolest way imaginable. "La-la Mademoiselle, my husband and la belle Madame d'Harcourt have gone away to philosophise together—doubtless—" then seeing my astonishment she said "Don't look so pained child. Are there no unfaithful husbands in your country?" With that she strolled away.

Though I am no prude, I own that I am mighty surprised at such Cynical Complaisance on the part of an injured Wife, and somewhat disgusted at the Hypocrisy of these French in general.

### August 16th

The weather so oppressive these last few days that no one has the strength to do more than stroll in the gardens, Philosophical conversation is at a standstill, the heat having exhausted what wits we have. I have hardly the courage to attend to my Journal, though to-day it is by far the best company in the place. 'Tis mightily hard to be good-humoured in this weather. This morning Madame d'Harcourt threw a plate at her page. My Father and Comte de Coligny had a heated discussion apropos of the British Crown Jewels which Monsieur de C. declares are mere replicas dating from King George I., the originals having been stolen by the Stuarts. My Father though in truth no very staunch Hanoverian, considered this a slight on the national honour and all but gave Monsieur de C. the lie direct. Ned, whom I have scarcely exchanged a word with all the visit, declares he is near dead of ennui.

The ladies here, in his opinion, are all head and no heart. He supposes that they can be wooed like other females, but swears he cannot please them. Little Madame de Sechelles de Vautrin seems indeed to have showed him some signs of favour, but to his vexation turns off his compliments with epigrams which he neither understands or wishes to. Monsieur de Belisle is very genteel and polite to me, and expressed a hope that we should meet in Paris. Madame de Brinoy, on my informing her of this, warned me against the man, though why she should do so I cannot conceive, for he has shown me nothing but the merest politeness.

*August 17th*

Riding party in forest. Dinner served on ground. In evening "Phèdre" acted in theatre. Very wearisome in my opinion, but did not dare say so except to Mme. de B. who heartily agreed.

*August 19th*

Madame de B. is the most excellent company possible. She has told me all manner of witty tales about the Court and people of her acquaintance. In her opinion the late Mme. de Pompadour was not such a marvellous beauty, though she had a certain brilliance in her youth. Indeed, she cannot think by what fascination she gained such a continued power over the King. Mme. de B., when she saw her a few years ago, says she was pale and delicate with blue eyes and a sickly complexion, and no eyebrows or eyelashes to speak of; and this last we agreed is a hideous defect in a woman. Madame de B. herself is blonde, but possesses pretty fair brows and grey eyes full of sprightly Laughter. Madame de P. also it seems had false teeth and an awkward manner. Madame de B. declares that a certain style of Ugliness in a wicked woman is pleasing to the opposite Sex, which seems a very wrong thing indeed. It seems that everyone is wondering who will fill the post of Maîtresse en Tître left vacant by the decease of Madame de Pompadour. Madame de Brinoy who combines Liveliness with Good Sense, thinks it highly ill that France should be governed in this manner by dissolute women. "The People," she informed me to day with a Grave air, "are starving. What can they think when they observe the Folly and the Luxury of the Noblesse."

In the evening here the guests sing or recite for the entertainment of the others, and I observe that the french perform in public without a trace of Shyness. The Duchesse begged me to sing, so I gave the company an Irish ballad on the Battle of the Boyne, and then a little shepherd song in their own Language commencing "Maman, dites moi ce qu'on sent quand on aime." Was much applauded and all exclaimed on the feeling I threw into the words. Indeed, my thoughts were with dear D. A. all the time I sang. Madame de B. is instructing me in another little bergerette entitled "Ah que ma voix me devient chère Depuis que mon berger se plaît à l'écouter," which she informs me was a great favourite of the Defunct Pompadour.

*August 23rd*

Among the guests here is a young Abbé of 17, who must truly be the most Lively Cleric in the world. He is a Beau Garçon, rides, sings, dances and makes Love to perfection. In short takes his spiritual duties very easily. Also an old Marquis de Dunfort who keeps the Company in shrieks of merriment Malgré Lui. He is as ancient as Noah but thinks himself a very great Beau and Lady Killer indeed. He attires himself sumptuously but in the mode of Louis Quatorze, viz: great red heels, huge scented wig, amber cane like a Maypole and ribbons. He will discourse for hours if permitted upon his Antique Gallantries, and carries a portrait of Madame de Montespan in his Snuff box. The young Abbé (who by the way is said to be the Fils par Aventure of a very Grand Personage indeed) asked him jestingly if he had ever been au mieux with Gabrielle d'Estrées, which made him very vexed! He declares that Ladies nowadays, dress, speak, and make Love like Servant Girls. This old Monster, strangely enough, possesses a young and lovely wife. This morning he insisted upon taking the air with me, and so we strolled in the garden, he pretending to give me his arm with gallantry but in reality leaning heavily upon me. We had paused for a second to admire a statue of Eros, and he was entrain of informing me what a Mad Success he was with the fair Sex, when we overheard his lady from a bower saying in a clear shrill voice, "Ah, chère Madame la Duchesse, les vieux Maris, le mieux qu'ils ont à faire c'est de s'en aller" at which I near split with laughter.

### August 28th

The days pass here in such an Agreeable and yet Trivial manner that I have found nothing to record of late in this book.

Among the recent guests are Madame la Marquise de Montfleux and her daughter, who is but 15 and a captivating Blonde cendrée. The latter very agreeable to me. She has but this moment left her Convent and is to wed soon a wealthy Widower of 50, whom she has never even set eyes upon. To my amazement she contemplates this Frightful Fate with Tranquility. The marriage de convenance here is the general custom. If I had been a frenchwoman Papa would have wedded me to Mr. Sutcliffe in a twinkling of an Eye, so thank Heaven who saw fit to have me born in Co. Down. Madame d'Harcourt came down this evening her head covered with gold powder. A mon-

strous spectacle, for she is a brunette and nothing could
become her more ill.

### September 1st—Near to Chateaudun

Nothing could be more Filthy than this Inn. The Food
indeed is excellent but the furniture is scanty, and the
windows and doors will not close unless Marie Bonheur
and self put all our weight against them. Indeed, I wish
I was in my sumptuous bed at Chanteloup. Parted yesterday
from our kind hosts with many Compliments and Thanks.
Madame de Brinoy on parting presented me with a pair
of captivating hyacinth earings and I am to wait upon her
at her hotel in Town. To add to my discomfort the room
next to me is occupied by a Dead Corpse. The landlady's
son died yesterday and Marie Bonheur, on entering the
Chamber of Death broke into Fearful Screams. Papa says
women are Damned Fools and how can a Dead body harm
me, but I wish to Heaven 'twas not so plaguey near.

### September 2nd—Chartres

Thankful to have arrived at length at this fine Cathedral
Town for we have had a cruelly Unpleasant journey. Last
night we were caught in a Thunder Storm, the rain fell in
torrents with most alarming flashes of Lightening. Our
wheels stuck fast in the muddy ruts. In short, we were glad
to ask for shelter at a Farm House, for we were far from
any inn or town. The owner of the farm was mightily surprised at seeing persons of our Quality and Nationality on
his doorstep at that time of night, but his wife hastened
forward and declared that she would be overjoyed to give
us Hospitality. Exhausted as I was, I could not help observing the Poverty and Squalor of the whole place, for the
kitchen, though moderately large, was almost devoid of
Furniture, no glass in the windows, rain leaking through

the Roof and so on. So utterly different from the Prosperous dwellings of my Papa's tenants in Co. Down, which are almost without fail Warm and Clean, with a Ham or so hanging from the Rafters. The children too, a small army of whom swarmed over the floor, were dirty and bare-footed. Marie Bonheur in great high Feather informed our good Hostess from what I could overhear, that we were English Princes of high rank and so we were treated with great Egards. Rickety chairs were brought forward, children were hurried out of the way. The son of the house produced a Hare and offered to let us eat it for our supper, praying us to say nothing about it, and making a great to do. Ned and my father at length discovered that he had shot it on his lord's capitanerie, and for this Trivial Poaching crime could be sent to the Gallies if he were discovered. Papa not only promised silence but gave him a Louis in exchange, which sent him into Raptures. The Seigneur appears to have power of life and death in this land. Our host's pretty daughter had an infant at her side more decently attired than the others which she displayed to me with some pride, but I could not comprehend her Patois. Marie Bonheur explained to me later that this Infant is the result of Droit de Seigneur, a Curious privilege of the nobility which modesty prevents me describing more fully. Spent night on a hard bed. Ned and Papa in chairs. The Family, I imagine, on the floor or in cupboards. Set off this morning in the fashion of a Triumphal Procession. The peasants generously rewarded for our night's rest. The children ran after our coach for sous, which I threw them out of the window. To-day being the Sabbath, the population here are all hastening to Mass. My father desired to read some sermons to Ned and me, there being no Protestant church here, but when the time came Ned was found to be gone, no one knew where.

## September 6th—Paris

My father has secured the services of Madame Dupont, an excellent, good-humoured female, to be my Companion. Madame la Duchesse recommended her as she is the Widow of her nephew's tutor, so I believe she will fill the Faithless Mrs. Stewart's place very tolerably. Paris very empty as yet, but I am glad of this, for 'twill give me leisure to observe it before I am plunged in a social Bustle, also to replenish and titivate my Wardrobe. Marie Bonheur, like all Parisians, has admirable taste and will advise me on the matter of caps, hoops which are worn here in moderation, and perfumes. I do not wish to proclaim my Insular nationality too plainly by my general appearance.

No letter from Mr. A. though I will own I had fully trusted to find one from him at M. Lafayette the Banker. This is excessively Vexatious. Surely he cannot be already Weary of me. I am apprehensive lest my last letter was in some way or other foolish, too complaisant or perhaps not affectionate enough to please him. Lud! How these villainous men are Capricious.

## September 8th

We are very well pleased with this house which is situated in the Faubourg St. Honoré and is commodious with a fair sized garden, Spacious rooms and long windows. Fine furnishings and Mirrors enough to satisfy a Narcissus. On the other hand, 'tis not over clean and would doubtless be hateful in the cold season, but this must be borne with.

## September 11th

Waited on Lady Hertford the wife of our Ambassador here, who received us with the greatest Courtesy. She has promised to present me to their Majesties and puts herself

entirely at our Service. The streets of this town are Vile
and Dirty after London, and monstrously narrow for the
crowd of noblemens coaches and chairs that throng them.
Some even in the good quarters of the city are divided by
gutters, and so after a day of rain are like swollen torrents.
The houses are nothing but wood and plaster, and crumb-
ling to bits at that. The Palais de Justice and Opera House
fine, but most of the town stinks vilely, though to hear the
french talk you would think 'twas Paradise itself. The poor
people here attire themselves in Black and Lady H. says
'tis on account of the mud splashed up by the coaches.

### September 14th

To-day was presented to their Majesties, the King and
Queen at Versaille. My Lady Hertford and Madame de
Rochfort, my sponsors for the ceremony. I attired myself
in white Satin and wore my Diamonds, yet was not utterly
satisfied with my looks, for I have grown thin of late. Ned
so resplendent in Crimson brocade that I could not refrain
from whispering to him as we entered the Royal apartments: "I vow you should be announced as the Duke of
Portaferry, my dear Ned," which vexed the poor lad. The
ceremony of Presentation was as follows: We were named
to the King by the first gentleman in waiting, my name
being sent in first. His Majesty kissed me on one cheek,
and then after a second's hesitation saluted the other, but
did not utter a word. My father and Ned then presented,
and I passed on with the ladies to the Queen, where I
made a Deep Reverence. Was then hastened on to the
Dauphin and Dauphiness, Mesdames of France and the
young Duc de Berry, Comtes de Provence and Artois till
I vow I was sick to death of them all. Lady H. says the
King showed me great favour in saluting both cheeks, for
this he usually does only to Grandees, women of Quality
receiving the single Kiss alone. Notwithstanding, I would

gladly exchange this Royal Kiss for a Wink from the faithless Mr. A.

As to the appearance of the Royal Family 'tis easy described. Louis the Well Beloved is Handsome and Dissolute, the Queen, Marie Leycinska is an old Dowdy, the Dauphin is like a Skeleton, the Royal Daughters are plain and Clumsy, and the Royal Infants are sickly. Versaille is magnificent to a degree, but I was astounded indeed at the swarms of ill-looking mob in amidst all this splendour. Some sell their wares in the very antechamber of the King. The Picture Gallery, Orangerie and Gardens superb.

### September 15th

Ned declares that he is enjoying himself very well in this place. Indeed, he is abroad all day and night. He says 'tis the Liveliest Town he ever did see, and that the Boulevards are full of coffee houses, filles, music and noise and this needless to say, is exactly what pleases him most.

### September 17th

Cards and Supper at Lady H. French and English present. One of the latter, a stern old Dame by name Mrs. Forster, informed me that when She had performed the Grand Tour as a Child she had never lent back once! I swear I near replied: "Doubtless, Ma'am, that is why you are so stiff necked now." The french ladies talking of nothing but whether Rouge is permitted to the Devout by the Church, and of the scandal caused by some lady of high rank who has been conducting an Intrigue with a common Soldier. I am become a True Parisian now. I lie abed all Day and up all night.

### September 18th

Madame de Brinoy escorted me in her coach to the Rue St. Honoré to see the Marvellous Temple of Fashion there.

This street is the home of the Marchand des Modes, and
we occupied ourselves for near an hour admiring the little
Dolls and manequins decked out in the newest Modes. These
are sent all over the World, even to Constantinople and
other Barbaric spots. Dinner at Madame de B.'s Hotel.
'Tis furnished most elegantly. The chairs covered with
Rose Indian brocade. The carpet dove coloured with a
Gold fringe. Also a superb rug composed entirely of
Ermine fur—exquisite pictures by M. Greuze and
Boucher. Sèvres china all sumptuous. Many guests present.
Among others, Madame d'Egmont, Princess Talmond,
cousin to the Queen, and a Genteel young officer, Monsieur
de Guys, cadet of a noble house and a Relative of Madame
who paid me some little attention, fixing his fine dark eyes
upon me all the meal which we eat in a Paved Hall with
Frescoes and a pretty Fountain.

The conversation very Witty. Epigrams and Bons Mots
flying here and there. All Courtesy Itself to me except one
lady, who asked me in a mincing voice if I did not live in
a country where there was a Perpetual Fog and nothing to
eat but Raw Meat and Baked Apples. Whereupon M. de
Guys remarked quickly: "At all events Madame, I believe
you will agree that the damp Climate and Apples have
together given Mademoiselle a very beautiful Complexion"
which I vow was immoderately Gallant of him.


*September 21st*

A most Astounding incident occurred to-day. Returning
with Madame Dupont from the Barbers we met in the Hall
a young man of about 30 or so, attired neatly but "en
bourgeois." I should not have observed him particularly but
something in his entire appearance and figure seemed to me
immoderately familiar. I gazed at him for several moments,
attempting to call to mind where I had set eyes on him
before. He returned my glance apparently no less Intrigued,

at length bowed and passed out. Then I caught a glimpse of my own Person in a mirror, and it dawned upon me that the young man and me were as similar as Two Peas! I seized hold of Ned who entered at that moment and cried very agitated: "For Heaven's sake, Ned, who is that person who has this minute left us?"

Whereupon he explained in a low voice that he was no other than our half-brother! It seems in short, that my Father when in Paris on the Ground Tour years ago, fell violently enamoured of a pretty actress by name Clementina Denise and this was her son, hence the extraordinary likeness between us, both of us taking after Papa. Ned very vexed because my Father is determined to give the young man a large sum of money to enable him to obtain a commission in the French Army. It seems that Ned and my Father have had some sharp words about it, but I own that I feel a strong sympathy for this new relation of mine. To look at him I might suppose myself to be gazing into a mirror, while Ned with his carroty hair, which he inherits from Mamma, seems to me but a brother in name. Ned warns me to say nothing to Papa of this "Else, Miss," he said, "you will as likely as not get a Box on the Ear." This incident has caused me more thought than anything else on this tour.


### September 23rd

The French are a curious people indeed. To-day was invited to a party with Mme. D'Agesseau and arriving found that the Lady of the House had just been brought to bed. This plan of Turning a Labour into an Entertainment is quite novel to me. Took refreshments and played cards in an adjourning room with a grand company of guests—till my Hostess was safely delivered of a daughter, whereupon I retired home.

*October 2nd*

Have not wrote in this Journal for many days being in a mighty great Bustle these last few weeks. Yesterday Madame de Brinoy took me to visit Madame de Luxembourg. This lady was notorious for her gallantries in her youth; indeed Madame de B. tells me some wit made the following little verse upon her :

> "Quand Boufflers parut à la Cour
> On croyait voir la Reine d'Amour;
> Chacun s'empressait à lui plaire
> Et chacun l'avait à son tour."

which I think says all that need be said. But now she is a leader of Society, arbiter of Bon Ton, a Paragon of Propriety and 'tis as essential to be presented at L'Hotel de Luxembourg as at Versaille. In short her Sins are forgiven her. She is a small, quiet old lady, attired simply and modestly without a jewel and you would never suspect she had been such a great Rake. Madame de B. accounts for her great Succés and the Merit she has acquired in her old age, by her prodigious Sang Froid. A great number of the Beau Monde present. It would seem that there is no such thing as old Age in France, for women of more than 60 are as Frivolous, as gaily dressed and as sprightly as young females. Madame de Brinoy, though she has indeed a youthful Air, laughs mercilessly at these Evergreens as she names them.

"At my age," she declared merrily, "a woman should be given up to Meditation. Indeed, I myself find great Consolation in thinking of the Sins I might have committed but have not."

Monsieur de Guys present, and to my surprise Monsieur de Belisle with as philosophical an air as ever. He hastened forward at the sight of me but I had a Malicious Joy in showing favour to Monsieur de Guys which I believe vexed him. Monsieur de G. is a captivating Fellow, elegant, witty, with vast superiority of parts. We conversed together for some time on the state of France. In his opinion the K. should be deposed. "That cursed Butcher's Daughter thank Heaven, is dead," he declared, "but you will see we shall soon be cursed with yet another money drinking wanton."

He abhors the Jesuits and is deeply solicitous for the Poverty of the Peasants.

"We are dancing on a Precipice," he declared, "but I can see no end to it all."

He spoke also with scorn of the nobles of M. de Belisle's kind, who preach Revolution and Freedom and at the same moment send peasants to the Gallies for Trifling misdemeanours.

All this Serious Talk accompanied by Doux Yeux. Madame de Brinoy thinks highly of this young man.

### October 3rd

Papa attends Madame Geoffrin's salons. Her Lundis are for the Artistic and her Wednesdays for the Literati. He declares that he meets very Cultured persons there and diverts himself prodigiously, but thank Heaven I have ended with all Philosophy, being engaged in pursuits more suitable for my age! Madame G. is a Bourgeoise, and not in society and will not permit women at her Reunions, and I think she is wise, for conversations upon Atheism and the famous Encyclopædia are more suitable for old men in their Dotage than young and pretty females. It seems that the other night some guest read from their works, and glancing up perceived that the Entire Company were dozing, which does not say great things for the liveliness of it all.

To-day received a basket of late Roses from Monsieur de Guys and concealed among the Blooms a little note very prettily worded, assuring me that he received more pleasure from my Society than from that of any other Woman he knows, and saying some other vastly Pleasant things about my Person and Mind. I am not so vain as to Flatter myself that all this Praise is True, but I will own that this Graceful and yet Respectful Homage is very Gratifying at a moment when my heart is Aching at Mr. A.'s Perfidy. Apropos of that man, I have wrote him a short sharp letter in case my first note was mislaid on route, and I pray that this may bring him to his Senses.

### October 5th

A packet of English books from Monsieur de Guys, for I complained to him the other day that I had nothing to read. Among others Mr. Hume, Richardson and Mr. Walpole's "Castle of Otranto." Ned, who I believe has found himself a mistress by his Lively Air, declares that Monsieur de G. is catched by me.

### October 6th

Cards at Madame de B. Met Monsieur de G. who would not depart from my side all the time. Madame de B. winks at me merrily about this.

### October 7th

Monsieur de G. has presented me with a charming little dog named Chloe. 'Tis the Genteelest, Sprightliest animal I ever set eyes on, and will console me for the loss of my dear Victor. Apropos of dogs, on the bridges here, the Shoeblacks cry at one: "Ici on tond les chiens et coupe les Oreilles aux Chiens et Chats," but I will not permit my little Chloe to be snipped even to be Modish.

## *October 9th*

Marie Bonheur brought me a short curious little note to-day. 'Twas in French and unsigned, to the effect that someone more worthy of my Favour than that Foppish little Officer (Monsier de G.?) was prepared to lay his Homage at my Feet and so on, calling me "ma belle Divine Fleur Irlandaise," "adorable Mademoiselle," and other foolish Terms of Endearment. To my mind it must be either wrote by a Lunatic or some Fool, wishing to play a jest on me. The french are very Partial to Hoaxes of this kind.

Marie Bonheur can explain nothing, except that it was delivered by a Lacquais de Louage. Very droll and mystifying.

## *October 11th*

To the opera with Madame de Brinoy. Wore my Rose Brocade and carried a Posy of Artificial Flowers which are the Mode here. She fetched me in her Coach which is Elegant like all she possesses, and has running footmen and Danish Hounds accompanying it. We were delayed for several minutes in a narrow street, whilst her Coachman quarrelled with another driver. She tells me that he is very particular as to Precedence, and would rather Risk overturning the Coach than give place to an Equipage of lesser rank. She herself is utterly indifferent to matters of this kind except when at Court. I informed her that Domestics were equally Odious in England, and recounted Paddy's Wicked Behaviour on the Bath Road. The music at the Opera poor, but the scenery sumptuous. Mademoiselle de Mesnils is the modish actress of the hour. Monsieur de Guys came to our box and stayed a great time conversing most tenderly with me. I wish to Heaven Mr. A. could know I have found another Beau.

## October 12th

Supped at Madame de Mirepoix. Saw Madame d'Harcourt as fair, as Languishing as ever she was. The lady has not the Strength now to lift a cup to her Lips or pull a bell rope—a lacquais must do it for her. Monsieur de G. very agreeable. Much diverted this morning at a street brawl below my Boudoir window. A woman emptied a Pail of Rubbish on the Head of a Priest, and then Lud! what a to do and yells and curses.

## October 16

It is with the Deepest Melancholy that I take up my Pen to record the events of this Unhappy Day. I went to visit dear Madame de Brinoy this morning. I found her at her Toilette surrounded by Acquaintances and Tradespeople. After a while she dismissed them and I observed that she was in a state bordering on tears. With a silent look of Grief she handed me a letter from Madame de Guys, the mother of my poor friend, near Distraught, and announcing that her son had been sent to the Bastile by a Lettre de Cachet. At first on perusing this Melancholy News, I was Ignorant enough to imagine that my Uunlucky Admirer had been thrown into prison for debt, and tearing off my Pearls, I offered them to Madame crying:—"We must make every effort to obtain his release," but Madame de Brinoy explained, with tears in her eyes, that this Dastardly business was the result of some Political crime or Indiscretion on my poor friend's part. What a vile country, where such injustices can be committed, and oh gracious heaven, what a Cruel ending to our Happy Friendship! Madame de B. hurried off to visit the Unfortunate Young Gentleman's Mother, and left me here. Have spent the Day in Deep Dejection. My father and Ned very solicitous, and Papa means to consult our Ambassador about this business, but I fear 'tis all in vain. I will be Honest and confess that Monsieur de Guys has not, and never could arouse in my bosom the Passionate Love which I even now feel for Mr. A., but nevertheless I have a Warm Regard and Affection for him. How can I fail to be Frantic at the Frightful Fate that has overtaken him?

## *October 17th*

Passed a Sleepless Night. Am deeply dejected. Have nothing but distaste at the thought of participating in the many parties and routs I have been invited to, but as Ned rightly remarks, If I display my Distress too ardently, everyone will Immediately conclude that I am poor Monsieur de Guy's chère Amie.

## *November 1st*

I see I have not wrote for a great long time. These last two weeks has been little else but a Weary Racket of Entertainments. The sad misfortune which overtook my poor friend has stolen all joie de Vivre from me, and I do not now enjoy these same gaities. I cannot say how I have missed his agreeable countenance and elegant person at these assemblies. The thought of him deprived of Freedom, and all that renders life dear, has embittered my stay in Paris, and I shall be happy to depart for Switzerland. Have learnt also that these Parisians are monstrously Selfish and Unfeeling beneath their masks of Courtesy and wit. Monsieur de G.'s imprisonment caused needless to say, a prodigious stir at first among his acquaintances, and all were highly indignant, but a few days passed and a Novel Topic became all the mode. All were laughing over the Scandal caused by some Cardinal or other who has been found to have a young female in his retinue disguised as a secretary in a Soutane, and so Monsieur de G. is forgot. I venture to mention the poor young gentleman to

4—TDOAYLOF

Monsieur de Tasse the other day whereupon he cried: "Oui Mademoiselle, c'est bien triste mais on n'en parle plus." Could anything be more Barbarous?

Last night a highly odious thing occurred to me. Ned and me and Madame Dupont went to the Opera. Papa being sick with the Gout. Half way through Ned spied a well-known courtezan, he is very catched by, and hastened to speak to the creature, leaving me alone save for Madame Dupont, who was asleep. Was mightily surprised when a second later Monsieur de Belisle entered my box, and sitting down by me without more ado began to make the most frantic love to me. Was so astounded that I remain mum like a Fool, whereupon he seized my hand and covered it with kisses. This vexed me furiously for I cannot abide a man with a badly turned leg, so I rose very angry, roused Madame D. and hastened away. The reprobate had the impudence to follow me even to my coach with Passionate Protestations, which to my Intense Mortification made the Bystanders laugh, and as I stepped in, the Insolent wretch said: "I believe you are amoureuse of that Idiot in the Bastille." This enraged me and I slammed the door in his face, pulled the cord and away we went splattering the Monster's fine coat with mud. These frenchmen are more licentious than could be imagined. Mr. A. is a Hermit beside them. My father mad with Ned for having abandoned me in this manner, and threatens to run Monsieur de B. through if he ventures near us.

### November 5th

I'll own I have reason to be grateful to Providence for I am convinced that I am a very Great Fool, and but for Heaven's special protection might be ruined through my own Folly. In short, last night I indulged in a Monstrously Foolish adventure which near proved disastrous. All the talk among the ladies of late has been of Alchemists and magic crystals, and I have for some time had an inclination to visit one of these Magicians, and see their wonders for myself. Marie Bonheur learning of my desire declared that she knew of a certain Italian Seer by name Signor Orlando, who could read the future marvellously well, and who was frequented by all the Beau Monde. She promised to make a Rendezvous for me at this Man's house last night. I will own I was drawn into this silly affair by the hope of learning some news of Mr. A. and Monsieur de Guy. I then thought for Greater Security and also to make the adventure more Diverting, that I would attire myself as a young man. In short, I took a green satin suit of Neds, and with Marie Bonheur's assistance cut it down to suit my figure. I tied my hair in a periwig and armed with a rapier and cocked hat, and looking a very proper young Beau, set off in a chair with Marie B. Arrived at the place, I was bowed up by a Negro Page to a dark room furnished with serpents and skulls. Waited for some time, Marie Bonheur having vanished, and began to be Uneasy. All on a sudden the page came in again. "In here, Monsieur please," says he and pulls back a curtain. I hastened into an inner chamber and came face to face with the detestable De Belisle, who grabbed me in his arms and began embracing me like a Lunatick. I will not trouble to write down all the indelicate and Abominable things he said. In a great fright I yelled and kicked and screamed. Thank the Lord, I had the good sense to draw my sword and deliver him a blow in the chest with the hilt, which made him leave go. Whereupon I ran out of the room, downstairs and into the road, and jumped into a chair and so home. Never has such an agitating thing occurred to me before. Papa knows nothing of this escapade, and never shall, if I can help it. The odious maid has never returned to-day. 'Tis plain she was in his pay, and besides playing me this Wicked Trick, she has stolen my Plum brocade, but 'tis not vastly becoming to me, and am happy to be out of this business too so easily.

## November 7th

I feel I must note down a diverting little sequel to the Alarming affair t'other night. To-day Ned, poor youth, decided to wear his green suit, which I had replaced by stealth, and was prodigiously Put Out at finding it too tight! The buttons strained to breaking point over his chest, and the sleeves too short. Needless to say I have not vouchsafed an explanation, and 'tis accounted for by the idea that he has grown Stout on french cooking. I laughed till near I split.

## November 19th

Very busied this last week with preparation for our prodigious lengthy journey. The Hateful Marie has been replaced by a Swiss girl named Nanette, who seems Honest enough. At all events she is excessively Plain. One of the valets very drunk, so we have found another. The journey to Switzerland will be very severe in this season, my acquaintances declare we shall never reach there alive. Have purchased a beautiful hood and cloak, lined with Fur, to keep off the cold. Also very elegant.

## November 22nd

We are to break our journey by lying at the Abbé d'Attune. Tom who was acquainted with him in Paris some years ago, has sent us Letters of Recommendation to him. We inquired at his Town residence, but they informed us that he has not visited Paris for many years now, and lives altogether in the Country, near Chalons. It will be agreeable to have this opportunity of observing true country life, for Chanteloup was magnificent, and in no way Bucolic.

## November 27th

Ned has purchased a Genteel little Mouse-coloured Donkey, who is to run behind our coach.

## November 28th

My last day in this Gay Cruel City. Our antechamber all in a Bustle with lacquais bringing Lettres de Congé. An affecting parting with Madame de Brinoy, who presents me with a sweet miniature of herself, set in pearls. She begs me to visit her on my return. Ned very vexed at leaving Paris. He seems to have an Intrigue with a lady of great fascination. At all events he is in a very Ill Humour.

## December 7th

Here we find ourselves at the frontier at Gex, and here we shall remain till we have recovered somewhat from the fatigues of our journey. My father suffers from sciatica, Ned has a cold in the Head, and I am for some reason or other excessively Low Spirited; melancholy at leaving France, yet unwilling to remain there, and Profoundly Uneasy apropos of Mr. A. Our journey was Damnably Unpleasant. The country we passed through was often Beautiful, but the incessant rain prevented me from admiring it. Inns vile, and one night I was obliged to have my bed in a kind of outhouse. Our visit to the Abbé though excessively vexatious to Papa was, now I come to think on it, the drollest thing that has ever occurred to me, and I shake with Laughter every time 'tis mentioned. After a lengthy day over bad roads we reached to our amazement a very Decayed looking house, more like a Ruin than a Gentleman's Residence; finding ourselves in a courtyard filled with rubbish, we concluded that we had mistaken our way, but the door opened and a Strange Figure attired in a Dirty Soutane, and carrying a gun, emerged

and glared at us like a wild beast. This it seemed was our
host the Abbé himself. He greeted us in a Surly manner,
declaring that he was occupied shooting wolves and seemed
at first inclined to leave us out in the Rain, at length led us
indoors—all very amazed at this Curious Reception. Never
shall I forget the amazing ménage we found ourselves in.
The house was filthy dirty, devoid of any ordinary Com-
forts. Seated in the hall were two men playing cards, as
Dirty and Unkempt as our host, ill-mannered country
Boors who did not even salute us, but continued to converse in Loud Tones. This embarrassed us, but more was
to come. A door opened and two females came out, both
painted abominably, and attired in Tawdry and Im-
modestly cut garments. They seemed angry at the sight of
us, and drew back. In short 'twas easy to perceive that
they were nothing better than common trollops. This then
was the home of the Benevolent and cultured Abbé, where
we had fondly hoped to lie the night! 'Twas all so Droll
and Unexpected that I near broke out laughing, but my
father became Purple with rage at finding himself in such
a low place, and when our host was out of hearing, he
declared that we must depart instantly. Ned and me however were near dead with travelling, and begged him to
remain, which he did, on condition that I should go at
once to my chamber with Mme. Dupont, and bolt my
door. We had a miserable repast of sour wine and soup,
my Father and Ned standing over me in such a manner
that none of our disreputable fellow guests were able to
approach me, if indeed they had desired to do so, for they
remained drinking in a corner, and plainly making lewd
jokes about us, and me in particular. Madame D. and me
were escorted by the Abbé, who all this time had not
addressed a word to us, to our chamber. Not a sign I should
say of a Domestic. To reach it we were obliged to cross an
open yard in the Rain, and so arrived wet and Shivering
in a Bare Room with not a stick of Furniture, but a bed,

a chair, and a table. We barred ourselves into this Delectable Apartment, and seeing no sign of water to wash with, lay fully clothed upon our bed, which to add to our Discomfort, gave way under our Combined Weights, and had to be propped up with the Chair. Needless to remark we did not sleep very soundly in this fashion, more especially as Loud Sounds of Merriment came from Below stairs, and also we were pestered by Lice. We were however unmolested though at about midnight a Heavy Body fell against our door, which we trembling concluded was a Drunken Guest retiring to bed. Papa and Ned woke us at Dawn, and we departed without setting eyes again on our Host and his friends. Papa more Vexed and Furious at this affair than I have ever seen him before. Ned and me inclined to laugh at it all, but my father in a terrible Passion. He declares that he would like to hang Tom for sending us to such a place—"My daughter lying in the same house as two wantons" he cried at least 20 times in a fury. He declares that he was a Fool to bring a girl on a Tour like this, and swore at me when I told him my Reputation could survive it. We inquired at our first opportunity for Particulars of our strange host, and an Innkeeper soon made all plain to us. The Abbé, though doubtless quite Comme il Faut when Tom was in France, is now a Notorious Personage. Some 10 years since he was banished from Paris for having wrote a Blasphemous and Obscene novel. He was in short Unfrocked and completely disgraced. He retired to the country, where he has lived a Life of Shocking Vice. No one will venture near him, except Disreputable men and *filles de joie* from the neighbouring town.

What could be more Ludicrous than that we should find ourselves in such a place? This morning Ned and self laughed over it, till we wept. I must own this Droll business has been a Welcome Diversion to my low spirits. I dreamt last night that Mr. A. was in the Bastille chained hand and foot.

# VI

# SWITZERLAND

*December 10th—Lausanne*

I am firmly persuaded that this is the most Idyllic country in the World. We had no sooner crossed the frontier into Switzerland than my spirits rose prodigiously. The air seemed more Salubrious, the scenery more Smiling, the inhabitants and houses cleaner, happier, and more prosperous than those we had left behind in France.

As I write from our hotel I can View from my open window what must surely be one of the Finest Spectacles in Europe. The famous Lac de Leman lies before me Blue and Sparkling in the winter sunshine, sailing vessels and other small craft gliding to and fro upon its Dimpling Surface, while upon the opposite shore are a Superb Range of Snow Capped and Craggy mountains, which seem the very guardians, stern but kindly, of this lovely country. No scene could be more calculated to cheer and yet elevate the mind. As I gaze upon these Awe Inspiring Rocks I am more than ever convinced of the Power of Heaven as demonstrated in Nature, and the Comparative Frivolity of our Human Desires and Efforts. The Food here is Excellent. 'Tis indeed a land flowing with milk and Honey. Nanette, who is overjoyed at finding herself in her Belle Suisse once more, brings me a Delicious cup of chocolate every morning and I dare swear I shall soon become quite stout. Indeed, I believe if I had stayed in France much longer I should have lost all my looks. We stayed at Geneva but a few days, for 'twas a large, Melancholy town, full of Pastors and excessively cold, and we were told that the air here is Finer and the Society more English. To-day walking abroad to examine the Town, I heard so many English voices around me that I might have imagined myself in Derby once more. 'Tis Delightful to hear one's own Tongue again. The streets here are monstrously hilly and Ill paved. I shall spend a fortune on shoes. A fine Cathedral and Castle here.

### December 14th

A pacquet of letters arrived from England. Ned received one from dear Cousin Noll, portions of which he read aloud out to us. At the end Ned cried: "Why, Sister, your villainous Admirer is at large!" but I gave him a sharp kick under the table, and Papa looked up sternly, which quickly silenced him. He informed me, as soon as Papa was away, that Mr. A. had left Ireland these last two months, and is in London with Sir James Ford. This news has agitated me more than I can say. It explains in some measure Mr. Ancaster's silence which has so Pained me, and yet I cannot imagine why, or with what Motives he has taken this step. How am I to communicate with him? What is he about? These and a hundred other doubts exercise my Troubled Mind. From what I have observed of London, 'tis full of Snares for a young man of Mr. A.'s hot disposition, and great good looks. I can only pray he will remain Faithful. I myself received to my Joy a letter from dear Lydia D'Arcy or Lydia Franklin as I should now call her. She is still at her Aunt's residence, but Fortune seems inclined to smile upon her. Her husband has lately become, through the death of a relative, second Heir to a Baronetcy, and so there is every Hope that her parents will be reconciled to the Marriage. Of this I am heartily glad. She begs me to send her some little Cadeau from Italy, which I shall most certainly do, and also inform her of the latest Parisian Modes. She declares she will name her infant Cleone if it proves a Female. We have moved to good Appartements in the Rue du Grand Chêne.

### December 16th

Several of the best English families resident here have paid us visits, and invited us to their parties.

This morning on the stairs a tall young gentleman with green eyes came up to me and bowing very respectfully, said that he had heard my name by chance, and was I any relation to Ned Knox whom he had known at Eton? When I owned that I was Ned's sister, he presented himself as Mr. Richard Dickinson from Co. Cork. Ned very delighted at meeting this ancient school-fellow. He is a very lively, genteel young man, and is out here to learn the language, though as he confesses himself, he has not spoken a word of french yet. I think he will prove an agreeable addition to our acquaintance. We took chocolate with him in the town, and he introduced Ned to a young Swiss lady shopping with her Mother. This young Miss, whom Ned appeared greatly to admire, is by name Mlle. Henriette-Cecile Pochon. She belongs to one of the genteelist families here. She is fair and handsome, her features agreeable and her person well formed. She responded to Ned's advances, but it is easy to see that she is modest and virtuous, and I do not know how Ned will care for that.

### December 21st

I am no less pleased with this place than when I first arrived. The admirable Simplicity of the Society here is most agreeable after Paris. There are many artistocratic families here, but I observe none of that Hauteur which is so Odiously noticeable in the French Nobility. In this blessed republic all are equally free, happy and self-respecting. Noble, peasant and bourgeois only vie with each other in serving the community. Still more marvellous, speech is utterly free and unrestrained. No Bastille threatens the Fortunate Swiss. The abuses of the French Monarchy are discussed and condemned at the literary and philosophical debates, all with the greatest boldness. Ideas, new and often startling are exchanged. The Rights of Individuality are proclaimed. Escorted by Ned and Mr. D. I have attended several reunions amongst our Swiss acquaintances, and I drew considerable applause upon my self the other evening by describing the poverty of the french peasant or of much of it as I had observed.

If I had made half these remarks in France, doubtless I would have been thrown into prison like poor Monsieur de Guys. The air of liberty which we breathe here is intoxicating, and there is a danger of throwing prudence to the winds and propounding wild and extravagant ideas, for everything one says is listened to with flattering attention. Lausanne is at present crowded with young Englishmen on their travels. Papa says that they are a Crew of Idle Young Puppies wasting their parents' substance; when they should be applying themselves to studying. But in my opinion they make the Society very lively.

Ned and me both out all day to parties where we dance and play cards. All the diversions here very innocent. The weather continues to be fine, though somewhat cold. This town is very clean after Paris.

*December 25th*

Though absent from Ireland and David A., to-day has been one of the most agreeable Christmases I have spent. The weather very fine and sunny and indeed they say that this is the mildest winter they have known for some years. The streets thronged with the bourgeoisie in their best clothes, all very merry and exchanging compliments of the season. Church, followed by a large dinner, which we gave here to our English acquaintances. Gifts were exchanged. Papa gave me "Excellent Discourses on Life and Death" by Dr. Giles Witherspoon, and a pair of red shoes with gold buckles. Ned, a china comfit box with apologies, for he is short of funds. Mr. D. presented me with a pretty pink embroidered neck-ribbon for dear Chloe. I gave Papa a Prayer Book elegantly bound, and a pair of fine lace ruffles to Ned. Many toasts were drunk, amongst others, The charming Miss Cleone—this to my vast embarrassment—and the Swiss Republic, in honour of our native guests.

Mlle. Pochon has had the goodness to give me a history of Venice which I shall study, doubtless with profit. I have offered her a length of fine Belfast lawn which most happily I had amongst my wardrobe, for I had not a sou left.

*January 3rd,* 1765

Delighted to receive a charming letter from dear Mme. de Brinoy. She expresses most kindly her regret at my departure and envies me my visit to this Country. She gave me a diverting account of a visit she has recently made to a country-house near Paris. The guests there were all young and immoderately lively, and spent their days and nights playing off tricks on each other, dropping salt in the coffee, pepper in the snuff, digging holes in the garden walks and so on. "At my age," she wrote, "one is not over-joyed to find a frog in one's bed." Apropos of poor Monsieur de Guys—she says that his friends are still active on his behalf, and she has strong hopes that they will obtain his release, which I heartily pray they may.

*January 5th*

I perceive that I never truly appreciated the Beauties of Nature before coming to this country, where we talk of little else. The Swiss delight in the majestic and sublime scenery which surrounds them. Mme. Pochon has, indeed, offered a gilded wreath of laurel leaves as reward for the most elegant poem on the Lake of Geneva, and though I shall not compete for this, I am every day learning the Infinite Superiority of Natural Beauty over the Gilded Hollow Luxury which is the work of Man's Hands.

Yesterday my Father, Mr. Johnston, Ned, Mlle. Pochon, Mr. Dickinson and me, made an excursion to the village of Clarens immortalised by Monsieur Rousseau in his sublime work "La Nouvelle Heloïse." This trip partook more of the nature of a Pilgrimage than a mere Excursion. Mr. J. and Mlle. P. in particular being ardent admirers of the celebrated writer. We performed most of the journey by chaise and the day being excessively fine and calm, we embarked near Clarens in a small boat, rowing by turns. Mr. Dickinson and I rowed side by side, my Father and Mr. J. in front with their backs to us. My oar slipped in my unskilled hand, throwing me violently against Mr. D., who took the occasion to kiss me. 'Twas somewhat sudden, but so respectful that I did not demur. Papa perceived something in the clear water, for he turned abruptly, but it was all finished then.

Ned and Mlle. Pochon, who were reading "La Nouvelle Heloïse" in the stern of the boat, observed this little transaction. Ned laughed, but I fancied I perceived an expression of Reproof on the face of the Miss. There is no question that though in every respect the Swiss are a vastly Respectable race, they are lacking in Sprightliness. We examined the village of Clarens with interest, and walked for some time in the Renowned Bosquet de Julie. Mlle. P. moved to tears at the thought of the unhappy lovers. Mr. Johnston also wept. Mr. D. showed great solicitude and led me away, and we plucked grasses and sweet smelling herbs. I have pressed the latter in my prayer-book. The scenery round us could be described by these words of Petrarch, which can be found in the "Nouvelle Heloïse :"

"Aux lieux des palais, des pavillons, des théâtres : les chênes, les noirs sapins, les hêtres s'élancent de l'herbe verte au sommet des monts et semblent élever au ciel avec leurs têtes les yeux et l'esprit des mortels."

We dined at an Inn and ate an admirable omelette. All very light-hearted. For our greater diversion we named each other after the characters of the novel. Thus Mlle. Pochon was "Julie," I was "Claire," Mr. D. was "Saint Preux" and so on. Was filled with admiration at the peasants who are tall, handsome and possessed of a natural breeding and easiness of manners. Their dwellings are clean and neat, nothing more unlike France could be imagined.

### January 8th

I have been begged to join the Société du Printemps which is a coterie of Young Ladies who meet together for Amusement and Instruction. The Male Sex are not excluded from this gathering, but there are no Duennas and 'tis astonishing with what decorum and propriety these same parties are conducted. Mr. A., in this company would be a wolf among lambs.

### January 9th

Mme. Pochon had the complaisance to escort us to Ferney to pay our homage to the illustrious philosopher, Monsieur de Voltaire. The great man received us in a chintz dressing-gown, with a flow of brilliant wit. Sometimes affable, more often peevish. To tell truth, he reminded me of nothing so much as a chattering old magpie. But we listened silent, with that Respect which is due to Genius, however Wearisome it may be. He related a variety of droll tales and spoke with immoderate abuse of Religion. This same subject it would seem is something of a mania with him. We had an excellent repast of fish and roast meat, and were later escorted by his niece, Mme. Denys, an ugly, silly female, round the house and village. Monsieur de Voltaire has showed the benevolence which he undoubtedly possesses beneath his Irascible and Odious manner in constructing dwellings for the peasants. Monsieur de Voltaire's house is simple but comfortable and genteel. It was filled with guests like an Inn. Amongst others an agreeable young painter by name Monsieur Charles. Mme. Pochon says his true name is the Chevalier de Boufflers. The country around Ferney resembles England but for a superb view of lake and mountains. Monsieur de Voltaire cultivates bees and cows. Papa thought highly of his farming qualities. The only disagreeable incident I have to record of this day's business, is that Ned, like the Damned Fool he is, attempted to engage in a controversy with our Illustrious host on the Influence of Religion on the Female Mind. The few words Monsieur de Voltaire vouchsafed to Ned in reply were of such a Savage and Mortifying nature that I near choked with Shame. We stayed the night here at a very good Inn in the Bourg de Four. We came to Geneva by barque from the village of Ouchy, to return tomorrow by the same route.

*January 12th*

A most agreeable party at the Société du Printemps. Several young ladies recited Odes of their own composition in praise of the Lakes, Mountains and other Beauties of Nature. Some more elegantly turned than others, but all displaying Sensibility and Refinement. Am astounded to observe how accomplished these Swiss Ladies are. Mlle. Pochon talked of nothing but a young couple of her acquaintance but lately wedded, who have retired to a chalet above the Lake and renounced town life and Civilisation in general. This Monsieur and Madame Ecuyer, although wealthy, live in Admirable Simplicity, milking their own cows, washing their own linen, in short, performing all Household duties without assistance. They eat no meat, nourishing themselves almost entirely upon greens, and, according to Mlle. P. are as Happy as possible. So joyous do they find their rural solitude that they have no inclination to return to Lausanne, but nevertheless are happy to receive visitors. A great many of their acquaintances have been to visit them this summer, and all exclaim at their bliss. To my mind nothing could be more Delightful than this kind of life. Would to Heaven that I could retire to some such Peaceful retreat with A Congenial Companion and pass my Days in Innocent Bucolic Occupations. After 2 Seasons spent in the gaieties of the Beau Monde, I am convinced of the Emptiness and Hollowness of what is termed Polite Society.

## January 30th

The days pass in the agreeabliest manner possible here. Ned has a fencing master and music-master two days a week, whilst I am engaged in studying Italian and Latin with Mr. Dickinson.

We have not, however, renounced more sprightly occupations! Last night we attended a fine Ball. Mr. D. and I danced a prodigious number of Minuets and French Country Dances. A vast number of English present. Amongst others Sir John and Lady Bower, Mrs. Templeton and her two captivating daughters. The elder Georgina is distinguished by the symmetry of her arms and shoulders. The younger Elizabeth, has, I admit, a killing enough pair of brown eyes, but her expression to my mind is insipid. Danced with Monsieur de Blonay, who owns, I am told, a fine château on the french shore of the Lake at Evian. He tells me that Amphion is a very fashionable bathing place now, and counselled Papa to visit it in the Spring for his gout.

Mr. Dickinson declares that some of the young English Gentlemen in Geneva have angered the Genevois who are excessively prudish, by their follies and excesses. Apropos of Mrs. Templeton, her absurd french is the laugh of the Town. The other evening at a party she was exclaiming on the cold of this country, and how she was constrained to sleep between two mattresses for warmth, but as she committed the amazing error of saying: "Il faut que je me couche entre deux *matelots*," the entire company was thrown into fits of merriment. I vow that if the poor lady had made the same blunder in Paris, her reputation would have been gone for ever.

### February 14th

Ned, Mr. D. and me escorted yesterday by Mlle. Pochon to wait on the Ecuyers in their rural retreat. The weather being at length favourable to this much hoped for excursion. The first part of the journey was by chaise. We were then conveyed up the Mountain Slopes, in sleighs. Monstrously cold, and I was near frozen notwithstanding my fur Cape. The E.'s Chalet is situated in a Commanding position overlooking the Lake, but not, thank the Lord, at an excessively high altitude, else should have been perished *en route*. Mlle. Pochon assured us that in the warm season the surroundings are Delicious, but now all under snow and a chill wind.

We found Monsieur Ecuyer brushing the Snow from the doorstep. Their welcome scarcely more warm than the weather, and it seemed that our visit was ill-timed, for our Hosts had been unable to lay in their usual provisions. They appeared vexed that we had not carried some viands with us. Mme. Ecuyer an agreeable, thin young female received us with amiability, but the repast we were offered was poor to a degree, being nothing but country bread and stewed roots. Ned, with his fine, healthy appetite and love of Roast Beef pulled a long face at such poor stuff. I near split with laughter to see his air of chagrin. Mme. E. waited on us all the meal like a common domestic, her spouse meanwhile declaiming on Monsieur Rousseau and the beauties of the Natural Life.

Observed that the poor lady's hands were all red and swollen, doubtless the result of washing dishes and floors in this inclement weather. The chalet commodious enough, but not over clean and in a great state of confusion. We did not stay long, for Mlle. Pochon and self were chattering with cold, and the two gentlemen had a sharp dispute with Monsieur E. on the Morality of Fox-Hunting. Monsieur E. declaring it was a sin to kill a poor dumb beast, Ned and Mr. D. defending the Chase with ardour. Monsieur Ecuyer to my mind an ill-tempered man who cannot abide contradiction. I vow I would not be shut up with him in the mountains for all the world. We made our adieux with readiness. I observed carved over the threshold the following words in french :

"Here Abides Beauty without Luxury,
   Peace without Idleness and Love without Sensuality."

Mr. Dickinson whispered to me in his waggish manner : "Indeed, Ma'am, I have never yet known a man who could be Licentious on Herbs and Water !"

Mlle. Pochon promised to wait on them in the Spring. "If," cried Ned rudely, "you are not frozen to death by then."

We refreshed ourselves with chocolate at an auberge, and never was drink more grateful.

*March 16th*

'Tis with regret that I contemplate our departure from

this Delightful Country where I have spent so many happy hours. Mlle. Pochon made a visit last year to her maternal aunt at Turin and declares to my surprise that she did not care for Italy. The towns she says are Dirty and Stinking, the inhabitants are Talkative and Untrustworthy. To-day Mr. Dickinson, who leaves to-morrow for Ireland came to pay his adieux to me. The young gentleman seemed somewhat agitated and sat for several hours conversing in a distracted manner. He declared that he had never been happier than during these last months in my society, and that life would seem very insipid when he could no longer see my charming countenance, and so on. At length he confessed that he had for some time been desirous of entering the Holy State of Matrimony, and I will own that I was fully expectant of a Declaration, when he ended all of a sudden : "Unhappily I have no Means but my Paltry Allowance, and even less Prospects, so I am unable to follow my Inclinations." Then pulling a piece of Eidelweiss from his waistcoat pocket he offered it to me, declaring that he had plucked it for me in the mountains, took a tender farewell and departed. I truly believe that the poor Youth is a trifle catched by me.

### March 18th

Am pained to have record that I had a monstrously sharp quarrel with Ned to-day, and thus broke my solemn vow made to Papa. I happened to fasten Mr. D.'s Eidelweiss on my bodice. Ned observed it and informed me laughing that Mr. D. was a damned liar and never climbed for it at all. I maintained that he had, whereupon Ned said in a provokingly rude manner : "My poor Sister, I was with him when he purchased it from a peasant in this very city." This threw me into a passion. Doubtless, 'tis unreasonable but I am provoked at discovering Mr. D.'s odious artifice.

# VII

# VENICE

*April 2nd*

Have decided on the following new wardrobe for the
Spring. Item. A buttercup silk, with red and green. White
Moire gown, ruffled with pink Lilac Satin, and a Striped
Peau de Soie. Pink and Apple Green Striped Satin with
Feathers. Crimson Gros de Tour trimmed with Valen-
cienne. Sky Blue Satin gown with Bouquets of Flowers
with thick Ruching.

This with what I have should set me up genteely till
Vienna. The Gentildonne here wear the neatest, prettiest
costume imaginable, which I should like to imitate, viz:
A three cornered hat worn over one side, a thick silk gown
and over it all a zendaletto of black or white lace which is
monstrously becoming to the face and form. Patches and
perfumes used excessively here and Nanette informs me
that the hairdressers are excellent.

Papa has purchased himself a new spring suit and as for
Ned, he is ordering himself new satin breeches and coats
every moment. Heaven knows who will pay for it all. The
Venetian ladies are monstrously pretty, and run about
the town as free as air, even the Noblest born. One of
them ogled Ned this morning and he near fell from the
Gondola with joy. He thinks himself in Paradise. Apropos
of the gondola, 'tis a most convenient mode of conveyance
and takes the place of a chair. One would be very uneasy
without them with all this Plaguey Water. We have a
gondola with a fine Canopy. Our gondolier wears a red
Hat and puts me in mind of Mr. A.

## April 3rd

To-day we paid our respects to several of the Noble Families here. The great families are the Moncenigo, the Gradenigos, Morosini and many others. Was astounded at the Magnificence of their Palaces. Hundreds of apartments, and Papa says he doubts if they have fewer than 9 gondolas and 50 servants in livery. The rooms hung with damask and cut velvet. Even at Paris I never saw such sumptuousness. They must be prodigiously Wealthy. The Venetian Ladies very affable and chattering about their lovers, the pains of confinement and clothes. They inquired eagerly of the latest modes in Paris. They offered me chocolate. All spoke french, happily, for my Italian is poor and halting. The mob have the strangest lisping dialect which I swear I shall never comprehend. Ned and me to the theatre last night, for the season ends on Maundy Thursday. They acted the "Diddone Abbadonata." The audiences conversed and laughed so loud before the curtain was opened that 'twas like Bedlam. A vast number of young nobles present in the Boxes with their mistresses. They spat on the mob below and conducted themselves in a very dégagé manner. The noble ladies some of them in very low dresses. In the tragic scene the heroine all on a sudden lifted her robes and danced a "furlana" and sang a popular song.

A masked youth threw a posy of flowers at me. Laughed to find among the blooms a note and written in Italian: "This girl would make Love itself in Love." We eat ices and chocolate between whiles. Have purchased a black gauze veil for a marvellously low price in the Merceria.

## April 4th

The churches very frequented by Society during Lent, and I have peered into Santa Maria Maggiore and San

Marco to-day. To my mind St. Marks can in no way be compared to Westminster Abbey. 'Tis small and dark and has a exotick Papist air about it which does not please me, though I will own the gilding is fine. Sermons being declaimed in both these churches, the congregation meanwhile sticking on patches, yawning and making Love very comfortably. A young gentleman pinched my arm with the Sweetest Smile in the world.

Papa furious at my entering a Roman Church but I assure him that it cannot harm my soul as I do not comprehend a word of their Latin Gibberish. 'Tis diverting and the Music often Ravishing. Ned plays at rackets and goes fishing with the young nobles here.

### April 5th

Good Friday so I stayed indoors and read my Prayer Book.

### April 6th

All the Ladies here have Cavaliere Servants or Cicesbeo as they call them here, and I shall be démodé if I do not procure one by some means or other. Madame Caterina Dolfin who has the finest gold hair and blue eyes imaginable, informs me that they are not Lovers so much as Admirers and are very convenient for holding one's gloves and are even willing to assist at one's Toilette. Fear Papa would throw such an Admirer out of the house.

Am kept awake all night by the Traccasserie below my window. A Traghetto there and I hear a Hunchback telling stories to the neighbourhood, Gondoliers singing Tasso or serenading their Belles, in short a continual Chatter till Early Dawn. Papa says he will move to a quieter place.

### April 7th—Easter Sunday

Ned and me watched a very Magnificent procession to

St. Mark for High Mass. The Doge in a Cambric hat and
golden robes escorted by trumpeters and other Pomp. Observed that he kept his hat on even in the sacred building
and this made Ned and me titter. A great crush, and the
heat and odour of perfumes unbearable, so we went on to
the Piazza and admired the Royal galley in the harbour.
Apropos of the Doge, he is a Mocenigo. The Dogaressa
Pisani Corner Mocenigo is they say, a very worthy lady.

### April 9th

Caught my dear Ned at his Pranks once more. Entered
his room for a moment, and on departing inadvertently
knocked over a screen which fell displaying a Pretty Little
Slut in a striped petticoat. The wanton curtseyed to me
and tripped out of the room, not in the least Abashed. Ned
very vexed and informed me that she was not a Fille de
Joie but a ballet dancer whom our gondolier has procured
for him. He then declared that he adored Venetian women,
who, in his opinion, were made for kisses, and would I
please keep out of his room in future.

### April 11th

Never have I seen so many courtezans as in this place.
They run around as Bold as Brass and are treated with as
much Egards as if they were women of fashion. They walk
on the Piazza hanging on the arms of the Nobles, and
every patrician's gondola has one seated under the felze.
Have even seen a priest bring his Lady love to church
with him. Believe the Venetians do not know what the
word "shame" signifies.

Ned says the Nobles here are the poorest spirited lot of
Jackanapes he ever met. When they are insulted they
merely laugh, and later hire an Assassin to revenge them.

Papa also declares that he is pestered all day by Poverty Stricken aristocrats begging him to give them money for the Ridotto.

In short they seem fit for nothing but Licentious Amusements. Lud! how Mr. A. would despise such poor creatures.

### *April 12th*

Paddy and Stefano the Gondolier had a fight to-day, and S. gave P. a black eye. Paddy very melancholy at first at all this water and no horses, but of late has taken to rowing a Gondola. Madame Cecilia Zeno T——n who is from all accounts a very lighthearted gallant lady, escorted me out to-day in her gondola. She pointed out to me an excessively handsome old noble who passed us and cried "That old gentleman mon aimable enfant, is father to all the handsomest young people in Venice." Madame also made me laugh by recounting to me a diverting tale which is going the rounds this week. It seems that old Madame Guistina Qu——i, who is among the noblest patrician ladies in Venice, has always been mightily severe on the younger and frailer members of her sex. The other day the poor dame found that her tiring maid who has been in her service, undressed her and performed her toilette for these last ten years, was nothing but a Man in disguise! All Venice is laughing at her Dismay, and needless to say not a soul will believe that he was not her lover.

Chloe is growing stout for the little wretch gorges itself on chocolate. My acquaintances each bring a sweetmeat for my cagnetta, as they call it, when they visit me at my Toilette.

### *April 15th*

Wrote a pretty little poem yesterday to Madame Contarina Barbarigo's tabby cat, but I have used it as a curl paper by accident and I have forgot how it ran.

Apropos of cats, this morning I read in the Nuova Gazetta or some such journal that a cat belonging to the parish of San Gervasio and Potasio had given birth to three black and blue striped kittens. Hastened to the barber where I found half my acquaintances, but the prodigious Cats had died overnight to our vast Chagrin. We took chocolate at Florians on the Piazza, and I heard all the Scandal. It seems among other things that Sir William Brock is ruining himself at the Ridotto. A vast amount of Theatre gossip, but it has slipped my mind. Listened to the organ in St. Marks. A gallant in a crimson cloak slipped a three cornered note into the bosom of my gown. The usual request for a rendezvous. Ned and me visited the Ridotto to-day. 'Tis the Gambling Saloon here and a strange sight indeed. All the gamblers masked, a noble at the head of every table of which there are 80 or 90. The place lighted by silver candles. All plainly in a vast state of agitation, yet all play in silence, their countenances alone demonstrating the uneasiness of their minds. Every kind of person here. Nobles and ladies of high rank, courtezans, beggars, Negros, Turks, Jews and cutpurses.

Ned informs me that the other night a noble staked his Mother and lost. I told him teasingly that I wished I could do the same with him !

### April 16th

A wedding shortly to take place between members of the Zeno and Conti families. Papa and me were invited to the bride's residence to admire the gifts she has received. A great banquet, and we spent over two hours examining her garments and jewels. Never have I seen such a wardrobe before. At least a score or more of gowns, all of rich materials. A profusion of gold and silver brocade, velvet, linen, fans, buckles, shoes, lace and embroidery. Among her gowns I call to mind in particular a superb costume of silver satin embroidered in silver and flowers, a cloak of rose coloured velvet trimmed with ermine and with a jewelled clasp, a mauve camelot riding habit embroidered in gold and silver, a gown of pale blue damask with bodice of beaver, a wrapper of blue velvet trimmed with Canadian marten, and all this for a Pale, thin girl of 16. It seems that many Venetians separate or obtain annulment after their marriages, and so as like as not, all this fine wardrobe will be wasted. Purchased to-day in the Merceria a white fan with gold sequins, a necklace for Cary and a lace cloak for Lydia Franklin. This cost me 15 sequins.

Saw in the Piazza a Russian officer with a blue and gold uniform, and a Turk in a Turban. Also observed a lady with a modish muff of leopard skin I should like to have the same. The Piazza is so crowded one can scarce move in it. I believe the mob live in it. Have persuaded Papa to dress our gondolier in a red silk jacket and sash and white shoes. The gondoliers at the traghetto wear plumes in their Hats.

### April 17th

A musical party at the Bonfandins. An abbé played superbly on the Harpsichord. Six charity children from the Ospedaletto attired in white with Pomegranates in their hair sang music so exquisite and Voluptuous that one lady in the company swooned from excess of pleasure and I will own I was moved to tears. Met a gentleman by name Count Zannetto, an elegant young man in a suit of lemon coloured Melodino. He attached himself to me with ardour, exchanging smiles and glances all evening. A strange, witty devil. Informed me that in his opinion Love should endure the space of a kiss, that he had made love to every woman in Venice, and that his mode of living was Messetto, bassetta, Donnetta. Then he presented me with his visiting card engraved with a Cupid and declared that he Adored me.

I laughed, and cried he was a Wicked Rake, but I will own I was reluctant to depart when Madame Dupont came for me.

### *April 18th*

Poor unhappy old Signor Dolfino has died of a Rage brought on by a Pert Niece.

Papa declares I shall kill him this way one day. We visited the Ridotto and I laughed to perceive Ned playing at Faro with a Lady with Coal Black Eyes leaning on his shoulder lovingly. Papa did not observe him. Doubtless Ned is running into Debt.

Stefano remarked to me to-day that I was killing the Gondola, I used it so often, and added that 'twas easier to watch a Sack of Fleas than a woman. 'Tis droll to observe how familiar the lower classes are with the Quality in this place.

### *April 19th*

A diverting Marionette Theatre in the Campo San Maurizio this morning. A Sacred procession passed by and all the crowd kneeled, leaving me upright, so I ran into an apothecary's shop and there met face to face my crimson gallant of St. Mark's. He bowed very courteously and escorted me to his Gondola, and thence to the Piazza where we sat and eat an Ice together.

His English as weak as my Italian, so our conversation confined to smiles.

A very genteel young man, and I gave him my lace handkerchief on parting.

A courtezan has her appartements overlooking our parlour. She sits in the window of evenings in a Deshabille très Gallant and combs her hair, and makes Sheep's eyes at Ned. Papa very Vexed at this, and pulls the shutters to with an Oath, to Ned's chagrin.

### April 20th

Ned and me strolling down the Calle della Madonetta this evening, when a window opened and a lady lowered a basket containing, to our amazement, a new born Infant! This was seized by a Gondolier who wrapped it in his cloak, sprang into his craft and rowed off without more to do. A strange City indeed.

### April 22nd

To-day to Murano to see the Convent. Invitation sent us by "Sua Eccelenza Abbadessa Reverendissima Donna Caterina Principessa Emos." Ned attired himself sumptuously in gold brocade, for he had heard that the nuns were excessively pretty, and have lovers. The convent parlour full of guests of high degree. The nuns many young and captivating seated behind a thin grille, wearing low dresses and jewels. Ned plainly catched by one of them, a creature with green eyes and blonde curls, who returned his doux yeux lavishly. Saw to my pleasure Count Z., with a party of noble ladies. I told him it was a pity to see so many pretty women behind bars—but he winked and assured me that they had not renounced the affairs of the world, or the Pleasures of Love by any means. He informed me that the famous monsieur Casanova had an affair with a nun in this very convent, ten or more years ago, but was imprisoned in the Leads for all his Licentiousness. Should not be surprised if Count Z. found himself there too. We have moved to appartments at the Regina d'Inghilterra for Papa cannot abide the racket beneath our windows.

### *April 23rd*

To a party given by some of the noble ladies here. There being only females, and no Gentlemen present, we drank our chocolate on the roof of the palazzo, and several of the guests loosened their hair. This bleaching in the sun they declare produces the auburn tint, for which the Venetian Ladies are so celebrated. One young lady sang to us very sweetly, accompanying herself on the guitar. We foretold the future with cards and exchanged gossip. Apropos of this it would seem that Mr. Houghton is so enamoured of Mme. Dejeune that he pays her four thousand ducats a year to keep her from his rivals. I should not have supposed her worth it, from what I have observed of her in the arcades.

The Contessa M—— cannot it appears retain her lovers because ... The ladies threw off all discretion and talked of their own love affairs, most freely. I heard things I could scarcely write down. This is indeed a gallant and loose city. I believe that poor Nanette and self are the only virtuous females in Venice

### *April 25th*

I met the gallant in the crimson cloak in the Piazzetta. He begged me most ardently to grant him the favour of a rendezvous to-morrow night. He swears on his Honour that it is to be nothing but a turn up the Grand Canal— which he declares is excessively beautiful by moonlight. He promises that it shall be arranged with utter secrecy, and that Papa shall know nothing of it.

### *April 27th*

Experienced last night a most Alarming and Terrible Adventure. My Imagination inflamed, and my Prudence overcome by the beauty and balminess of the night and I decided to yield to the request of my Beau. Attired myself in mask and cloak. Stefano, whom I had bribed, unlocked the door for me at midnight. Met my gallant as arranged in the little court behind this place. He embraced me tenderly, and was preparing to lead me to his gondola when the air was rent by a Fearful Scream. There was a Curse, a Splash and a Gurgle, and a gondola sped by us, in the narrow canal—in it a young female struggling for dear life. Perceived by the moonlight, to my Indescrible Horror, the corpse of a young man floating face downwards in the canal! I uttered a Shriek, we heard the sound of running footsteps, whereupon my Friend throwing his cloak over me whispered: "Quick, hasten home," and ran like a hare down the Calle. Thank Heavens, Stefano had the door ajar, and I stumbled into his arms near dead with fright. Revived by a glass of wine, I wept. S. informed me in a low voice that such midnight assassinations are not uncommon here. Thankful to reach my bed and lay awake all night in a tremble. Cannot forget that poor murdered body. No more terrible punishment could I have had for my Indiscretion. I vow I will never more embark on these romantic escapades. Suffered from the Vapours all day.

### April 29th

Poor Nanette is sick of the Colic. The foolish wretch had a pain in her head, and purchased a remedy from a quack doctor in the Piazza—and this is the result.

Apropos of Ills. I am astounded to see how sensitive the Venetian Ladies are to odours of all kinds. It appears that Mme. F. swooned this morning on account of a smell of frying, which penetrated from her kitchen to her chamber.

### April 30th

It would appear that this town is bristling with spies.

Ned finds that the little ballerina he has been conducting an intrigue with, is in the pay of the French. He has repented of his penchant on hearing this, and deserted her. Papa commends him highly for his discretion. Ned has also heard that the dead body of a priest yesterday night was found in a well near the Friari. It seems that such tragedies take place daily. Papa however declares that he has heard that the Inquisitors have but one spy. I recollect now being informed that the Comtessa P. was accused last month of having poisoned an Aged Husband and was soon after found stabbed in her bed. Some say this is an act of Vengeance. At all event very shocking. To a party where we played cards on a rug.

*May 1st*

Great rejoicings to-day. The Doge presented a bouquet of flowers to San Giorgio Maggiore. Ned and me watched the procession from the balcony. The road illuminated by torches, and the Dalmatian body-guard sounded their trumpets.

*May 3rd*

A fine regatta to-day on the Grand Canal. The gondolas all decked out with flowers and brocade.

There was a race of boats—sometimes females take part in these races. Many of the larger vessels magnificent as various symbolical objects, such as the Chariot of Juno, the Chariot of the Stars, the Kingdom of France, the Chariot of Love and so on. The gondoliers in superb habits. It seems that the State wish to suppress all this extravagance, and richness of attire on the part of the nobles, but these sumptuary laws have little effect, I believe. Justina Conti declares that there is an edict against false bosoms. These are imported from France, and are much in vogue among the slighter Venetian Ladies. The lower classes attire themselves richly here on festive occasions. The women wear skirts and bodices of bright hues, white slippers, gold chains and pretty ribbons.

The bourgeosie it seems are more sober in their costume and manner of living. To-day I went to the Rialto where all the merchants live. 'Tis a very busy industrious place, and stinks of tan. Purchased a fine water melon from a brown naked child.

## May 5th

Papa and me dined to-day with old Signor Nani. His palazzo is sumptuous. He possesses a fine library, and many beautiful antiques. We were surprised to observe a bust of Shakespeare, and it seems that our host is a prodigious admirer of the immortal Bard. We dined in a summer-house on the roof garden—the smallest plot of ground imaginable, but half the dimensions of the rose garden at Kearney. Signor N. monstrously vain of it.

It was so encumbered with antiques that it was near impossible to move about. One statue of Aphrodite very pleasing.

The conversation lively and witty, but the meal itself very frugal, as I have observed before now at Venetian parties. Signor Nani has recently printed, at his own expense, the works of Ovid. All the Venetians penning books, pamphlets and poems vigourously. The talk is all of the struggle between the nobles and the Ten, whom it seems are Tyrannical. Signor N. says 'tis easy for an enemy to slip a note of accusation in the Lion's mouth, and so bring about one's arrest. He informed us that the Nobles are ruining themselves at the Ridotto. One, the other day, staked all his garments, and had to return home naked. The Bourgeois assume the dress of Nobles, all of every rank are as dissolute as they can be, the zentildonne are nothing but courtezans, in short he was full of complaints.

We drank coffee, played cards, and heard music. Signor Nani presented me with an exquisite fan painted by Rosalba Carriera.

### May 6th

Conte Z. to-day asked me to become his mistress. Informed me that he had a sumptously furnished casetta waiting for me. Upon my refusing the honour he seemed very put out, and declared that Englishwomen were as cold as Dead Fishes. I informed him that I was enamoured of another man, whereupon he left me in a rage, crying that he had never been treated in such a way before.

### May 9th

A prodigiously tiresome to do to-day. Nanette came to me weeping and at length confessed that she had been seduced by that villainous gondolier Stefano, though why she should think it necessary to inform me of this Heaven knows. She wailed and vowed that she would never have left her beloved land had she known what a Licentious place I was bringing her to. Fear I scolded her somewhat sharply, for I cannot comprehend why such a Plain wench should not be virtuous. Papa heard the traccasserie, came to inquire the reason and flew into a fearful passion calling her a wanton, and every rude name imaginable, at which she wept the louder. Papa summoned Stefano and damned him furiously. The wretch had the Barefacedness to declare that such a clumsy girl should be thankful any man had looked Twice at her. At length I turned the whole crew out of my chamber and bolted the door.

The household has been thrown into confusion by this odious occurence. The porter, father to Stefano, fell upon his son and beat him with a stick. Papa curses the Venetians and the sex in general.

Met Conte Z. buying tarts in the Piazza. He bowed to me, not in the least abashed. Laughed heartily when I informed him of this business, and said 'twas only to be expected. Fear he has a wagging tongue, for hardly had we parted than half a dozen of my acquaintances asked me if 'twas true our gondolier had seduced my waiting maid. Am weary of the whole affair.

### May 11th

Stefano and Nanette wedded to-day at the Parish church of San Moise. Papa determined on this union, and the gondolier's tears and entreaties would not move him. Gave Nanette my flowered silk for the ceremony. I vow 'twas the most melancholy affair of the kind I have attended. The bride weeping with shame, the bridegroom very sullen. Happily, Nanette is a native of the Papist canton of Valais, so they are of the same Faith.

Many of Stefano's relatives and friends present, and they laughed and chattered throughout the ceremony as if they were at the play.

Stefano regained his natural liveliness of spirits somewhat after the nuptial repast, which we had spread for them, and informed me that though Nanette was plain she was well covered, and would doubtless prove a good housewife. Have doubts if this marriage will prove very felicitous, more especially as I have observed that some of the lower class Venetian females are excessively handsome, but Papa takes great merit to himself for having made "one female at all events Respectable."

### May 12th

To-day have attained my 21st year. Papa presents me

with an elegant rose satin cloak embroidered with golden butterflies, such as the Ladies wear here, a black mask edged with fine lace, and a pair of embroidered gloves, all this is preparation for the Carnival. Also he has given me a sumptuously bound copy of Goldoni's comedies, which I cannot read yet, but which I shall treasure as a proof of Papa's Esteem and Affection. Ned absent these last few days, and my father is very Vexed at him not being present for this Anniversary. Papa and self had a very touching interview this morning. Papa pleased to say that I have been a more Dutiful Daughter of late, and I for my part vowed not to vex him any more. Apropos of Sentiment I am wondering if Mr. Ancaster is thinking of me to-day, or if he has been False enough to forget the day of my Birth. I will own I am Mortified at having no word from him. If he could but know I have not thought of him overmuch of late, not from any inconstancy, but from the great Bustle I have been in. The days pass here in a most agreeable trivial manner. Have not opened a book or lifted a needle for weeks. The mornings I shop in the Merceria, drink chocolate and gossip; afternoons, visits and gossip; evenings, parties or trips in the gondola, and more gossip again. Scandal and talk of clothes occupies my time. Am continually running around to see the sights. I wear out a pair of slippers in a week here. Never have I been more light-hearted, and I vow I shall be monstrously sad to leave for Vienna.

Conte Z. sent me a lovely bouquet of flowers to-day with the inscription: "To my Virtuous but ever adored Cleonetta." Several of my acqaintances have brought me little gifts.

Lucrezia Reni was malicious enough to say "What, 21 and not yet married!" Papa also mentioned that he had received a letter from Mr. Sutcliffe who hoped to pay his respects to me on our return.

Lucrezia Reni declares that Madame Maria Gla——go

has given birth to a monster. I could scarce believe this, but she swears 'tis correct. Her maid was informed of it from the maid of the lady's sister. This woman declares she helped to tie it in a sack and throw it in the Canal. Could anything be more shocking?

## *May 16th—Feast of the Ascension*

All Venice En Fête to-day, from earliest dawn for the Festival of the Betrothal of the Adriatic. Was woken up at 4 by singing and shouting below my window. Papa and me and Ned attired ourselves in our gayest garments. Had vast difficulty in making our way to the Gradinigos palace, the Canal so thronged with craft. Partok of a light repast with our hosts and entered one of their gondolas in which they had been aimable enough to allow us places. Thus we had an excellent view all day of the Festivities. The G.'s gondola draped superbly in gold brocade, fringed with purple, their ladder embroidered in silver upon either side. Their gondoliers in rich costumes, the oars gilded. I lay on cushions of purple satin and thanked heaven I had on my Lilac satin and Pearls for this Festive occasion. We made our way laboriously in the wake of the Bucentaur, which is a superb gilded state vessel, and had the satisfaction of seeing the Doge perform the ceremony though from a distance. The water covered with craft of all kind, Warships and merchantships decked in flags, gondolas, feluccas, galleys and skifs. Indeed, I believe, one might have walked to the Lido over the water without wetting a shoe buckle by stepping from boat to boat. The finest day possible. Bells ringing and tapestry hung from all the windows. I swear I was utterly confused by the brilliance of the scene and Papa declares he has never in all his life seen anything so fine. Everywhere was a field of jewels, brocade, flowers, pearls, and fans. An incessant noise of music and cries from the gondoliers. Numerous quarrels and heads were broken.

A banquet given by the Doge in the Palace. A table laid with rare fruits, sweets and wax ornaments. The mob admitted to this in masks. Ned and me with a great crowd of people waited to see the marvellous clock on the Tower. On the stroke of the hour a door opened by the Madonna's Throne, and a procession of angels and wise men came out walking like live people. Never have I seen anything so ingenious and cunning. I cannot think how 'tis done.

To bed now vastly late, my head in a buz.


### *May 17th*

Carnival commenced yesterday and this place is gone Mad. All masked from the Doge to Stephano and every vestige of Discretion thrown aside. The city is in an uproar. All work is at an end. Day and night equally Lively, and cafés open from dawn to dawn. My pen cannot describe the License and Jollity which reigns. Papa, in view of the general confusion, ordered me sternly to keep within doors unless escorted by Nanette or a domestic, but there is no such thing as Rule or order now, and I slipped on a cloak and mask over male attire (breeches and coat of rose satin and sulphur waistcoat) climbed down the balcony into a gondola, and so away! 'Twould keep me up all night if I were to note down all the curious sights I have seen.

The Piazza is filled with booths and stalls and high poles with banners, and a crowd so thick that I was near pressed to death. I vow there must be thousands of foreigners now in Venice. A mass of singers, acrobats, fortune tellers, dancers and clowns. Saw a panther and an elephant by the Ducal Palace, and to my vast amazement an Irish dwarf (or so they called him) for when I asked him what county he came from he could not comprehend a word! 'Tis as well my morals are not as loose as poor Nanette's, for I could have found occasion to-day for a score of Amorous Adventures. A quantity of Masqueraders begged me to enter their gondolas, and my arm has been pinched and pulled till it is Black and Blue. Kisses are plentiful but the Mask is mighty convenient, for it does away with the need to blush. Took me an hour to return from the Piazza to this place. Experienced some odious little adventures, and was constrained to draw my little dagger now and again.

### May 18th

Ned and me to the play. A ballet and the dancers threw themselves into strange contortions. The town lighted by lanterns and gay ribbons stretched from house to house.

To a party at the Testas. We proceeded round the town in Gondolas hung with jessamine, and singing barcarolles and serenades. This gaiety lasts for 2 weeks. I swear I shall be worn to a Shred by the finish, for 'tis near impossible to snatch a Wink of Sleep at night, with all the sounds of Merrymaking.

### May 20th

'Tis damnably hot now and I feel somewhat in a fever what with all the Buz and Racket of these last few days.

Last night tossing on my couch, I could have sworn I heard a familiar voice singing beneath my window. Ran on to the balcony but saw nothing but a gondola rowed by a tall masked figure, passing by in the light of the moon.

'Tis Droll what strange tricks an overheated Fancy will play upon the Mind! Ned away once more. Papa declares this town is like a Madhouse.

### May 21st

Il Travestito has commenced. Even my father owns 'tis diverting to observe the various costumes. 'Tis indeed enough to make one split to see them. Saw to-day in the Piazza a Bear on a Wooden Horse, a Devil and an Archangel all in a few seconds! Anything however droll will serve as a disguise, a Pig's head or a pillow case worn on the head. Some of the females wear moustaches, while the men garb themselves as courtezans, old women and so on. Watched a tight rope dance in the Piazza. We met Conte Z. attired as an Ape. He informed us that one year a patrician Lady performed on the rope in the Public Gaze. We purchased biscuits and fruit from a hawker. To an assembly at the Crimani. Attired myself as Hebe. Some monstrous tasteful rich costumes.

### May 22nd

A Most Terrible Catastrophe has fallen on us! My hand trembles so with Indignation that I can scarce pen these words. No more frightful contretemps has occurred to us on these Travels, and I feel deeply the need for some Sympathetic Female to whom I could confide my Fears and failing such a person I must again Fly to my faithful Journal. Am Thankful poor Dear Mama is in Heaven and not able to see the Disgrace her favorite child has brought upon us.

In short that Damnable Intolerable Fool Ned has run off with a Nun! It seems that he has been conducting an intrigue with her for some weeks, indeed since he first set eyes upon her that day at Murano. Yesterday with Unpardonable Foolishness he attempted to elope with his Flame. The Baggage escaped from her cell, and the 2 wretches took gondola to the mainland and so hoped to fly to Geneva and be married. Their flight was apprehended, they were pursued by the lady's relatives and overtaken. She has been flung once more into her Convent and poor Rash Ned has been arrested by order of the counsel and is under lock and key.

Our first intimation of this horrible business was this morning when to my Alarm a party of State Officers entered the house and conducted a search of Ned's room. Papa was away, and I thus learnt of the alarming fate which has overtaken my Unhappy brother. They departed after having sealed the escritoire, and all Ned's boxes. My father found me weeping on the ground amid Ned's scattered garments. Informed of the disaster he unlaced my dress and administered Smelling Salts with touching Solicitude, and hastened away by Gondola to the British Ambassador.

He has not yet returned and I am in a Terrible Tremble. Gracious Heavens, why did not Ned's inclination lead him to ballet dancers and courtezans? Sure there are enough loose women in Venice if he must be dissolute, without him ravishing a Cloistered Nun.

It would appear that what renders his crime more grave is that his love who is but 14, is a member of one of the highest Venetian families and a daughter of the Golden Book. I swear I dare not write the name in this book so illustrious is it, and there is every possibility that our belongings may be again subjected to search. Indeed I mean to keep this Journal under my mattress or in some safe place, lest an indiscrete remark in it should lead to my arrest. Stefano declares we shall be now under the scrutiny of the Inquisitors' spies day and night, and counsels me to keep within doors.

What seems to me so strange in this affair is that if Ned had merely continued to be the lover of this Nun all would have been well, for they are permitted to carry on intrigues and lead lives of great immorality; but to attempt to become her lawful husband was it seems an Unpardonable Sin, and thus poor Ned is to suffer for the first Respectable thing I have ever known him do! The lady in question is an heiress whose wealth the convent doubtless expects to inherit, and this I fear will make their vengeance upon Ned the more Ferocious. As for her Papist relatives 'tis plain that her crime in their eyes lies in her having brought open scandal upon them in attempting to wed a foreign heretic.

A small crowd has been around this house since the dreaded Inquisitors' gondola was here this morning, and 'tis enough to keep me indoors, for in my present condition of Agitation I have not the Courage to subject myself to the Laughter and Remarks of a Venetian crowd. Lud! I am too weary to write a word more.

## *May 23rd*

We are still in the Deepest anxiety with regard to the unhappy Ned. Papa is at our minister's day and night now. We are highly apprehensive lest poor Ned should be confined for months in the State Prison, like poor Monsieur de Briand who was 10 months in dungeon below water, and was released only to expire of a slow fever. Papa says at the best we shall be obliged to pay immense sums to obtain his release.

The news of his escapade has spread all over Venice. Many of our acquaintances including the Manins, the Loredans and the Bonfadinis have called on me to-day to satisfy their Curiosity and express their Condolences. Most are Affable and Solicitous but one or 2 were excessively spiteful, in particular Lucrezia Reni and Maddalena Sarbellon. Indeed I'll own my Deepest Shame arises from the fact that a member of my family should have repaid the hospitality offered us here in such a Base manner.

It seems that Signor S—— who is a member of the Senate and was so agreeable to us at at the Rout at the Barbaro, promises to assist us with regard to Ned.

### May 24th

Papa interviewed to-day the father of Ned's charmer. He returned deeply dejected and informed me that her relatives are enraged, and determined to avenge themselves upon Ned. Papa is making fresh efforts with our English minister.

Paddy in a great Melancholy. He has ceased cursing Stefano and tells his beads all day long now.

### May 25th

At the Ambassador's intercession Ned has been moved to a larger cell, and I was permitted the melancholy Pleasure of sending him a few necessities. He sent a message begging for some clean linen and books. Madame Dupont and me prepared a box containing the same, and I added some pastries, a flask of wine, a snuff box and one or two lively novels which I pray may cheer the unhappy reprobate.

Also sent pen and paper with which he is to write a full Confession, to lay before his Judges at his examination. 'Tis a thousand pities I cannot write this for him, for his Style is very halting.

The Carnival continues with unabated Vigour but I, needless to say, take no part in it. Would to Heaven it were over, for the incessant racket drives me near Frantic.

### May 26th

Papa saw Ned to-day. The poor youth he reports as being Deeply Dejected.

Signor N. has had the goodness to counsel my father to wait upon Madame Margherita Trami, the mistress of a Most Important Personage. This woman, he declares, if presented with a handsome gift might be more Efficacious in obtaining Ned's relief than all the efforts of our Ambassador.

Papa has a rendezvous with her at her house this evening, and commissioned me to purchase a present got her in the Merceria. Decided on a handsome pair of pearl and enamel earrings, which should excite the creature's cupidity and gratify her Vanity, and so lead to good results.

## May 27th

To-day the Inquisitors sit upon Ned. We are in a Terrible To Do. 'Tis now four o'clock and no news has been heard, though Papa, Paddy and Stephano are waiting in the Antechamber. Lord help us!

## May 28th

Heaven be blessed! Ned is to be released and will be returned to us in about 5 days. Papa and me on hearing the Joyous Tidings near wept with Pleasure!

'Tis indeed delightful to feel that our Tribulations are at an end, and that the poor wretch will soon be at Liberty.

'Twas late last night that Paddy and Stephano returned post haste with the glad news. Papa and Signor Nani later. Papa is to pay £200 in sequins to the injured parents, and £150 to the convent. Ned's unhappy flame is to do penance. Shall pass a Calm Night at length. Monstrous relief. Great rejoicings in the houschold! Paddy ceased telling his beads and renews his swearing at Stefano. Papa says we must leave for Vienna the very day Ned is freed, lest the relatives of the nun, who are still Indignant, should wreak some vengeance upon him.

Must interview Rosina apropos of a Travelling Gown.

I must not only put up my own belongings but also overlook the packing of Ned's wardrobe.

## May 29th

Stupendous Discovery! Mr. A. is in Venice.

# ENVOI

Miss Cleone Elizabeth Knox's Journal ends abruptly here. Fortunately, I have been able to trace her subsequent movements from a voluminous correspondence which has been preserved in Ned Knox's family, and is still in the possession of his descendants.

Mr. David Ancaster had evidently left Ireland some months previously on account of a duelling escapade, and had been travelling on the Continent with Sir James Ford. He had arrived at Lausanne on his way to Rome, and hearing there of the movements of the Knox family, had left his companion and followed them to Venice.

There, as seen in the Journal, he got into communication with Miss Knox. A tradition in the Knox family is that he made his presence known to her by singing an Irish ballad under her window.

The lovers decided to elope before Cleone was taken away to Vienna by her father, and five days after the last entry (June 3rd) they left Venice together, taking with them Nanette, the maid, her husband, Stefano Scomparine, and the dog Chloe.

Miss Knox, one gathers from a letter written to her some weeks later by her brother Ned, left most of her personal belongings behind, including her journal. Ned Knox promises to send her "your beloved Diary," but he probably never did so, for it was rediscovered in 1904 among the Knox family documents.

Old Mr. Knox, as would be expected, was very angry at his daughter's action. The state of mind he was in can be deduced from answers to letters of his written to various members of his family.

Tom Foley, his son-in-law, sends from Derbyshire four closely-written pages of condolence.

"Cary and me," he writes, "are more Agitated and Distressed than we can say at this unforeseen Catastrophe. We beg you, dear sir, to calm your Outraged Paternal Feelings, and put your trust in Heaven, who in its Goodness will surely not permit our beloved sister to be utterly ruined by that Scoundrel Ancaster."

He also confesses that he and his wife had always felt doubtful as to the advisability of exposing "a young female of C.'s lively disposition to the Temptations of the continent." The fears which Mr. Knox and his family evidently felt were fortunately groundless.

Mr. David Ancaster and Miss Cleone Knox were married ten days after they left Venice, in the Protestant church at Geneva, by Pastor Getay.

From Switzerland they left for Paris, where they remained a fortnight with Madame de Brinoy de Chateauroux. A letter of hers to Mr. Knox, written, no doubt, at Cleone's instigation, assures him that *"vos chers enfants sont follement heureux"* and begs him to forgive them.

This letter is addressed to Vienna. In spite of the elopement, Mr. Knox and his son do not seem to have altered their plans for their Grand Tour. The young couple then returned to London, where they awaited Mr. Knox's return. Unfortunately, no description has been found of the interview between Mr. Knox and his new son-in-law. There are various other letters written at this time and relating to the episode. Three are from Mr. Knox's lawyer in London on the subject of Cleone's fortune, and pointing out to Mr. Knox that he could not prevent her enjoying it now that she was of age.

There is also another letter from Tom Foley, thanking his father-in-law for the copy of Cleone and David

Ancaster's marriage certificate, and a facetious one from Cousin Noll, who is mentioned in the journal and who was Mr. Oliver Knox of Ballywiticock House.

Mr. and Mrs. David Ancaster returned to Ireland in the spring of 1766 and settled down at Castle Ancaster, Co. Down. The relations between the two families seem to have been rather strained at first, but after Cleone had presented old Mr. Knox with two grandsons, he evidently became completely reconciled to her and her husband.

Ned Knox married in 1769 Miss Bullen, an heiress, and Cleone Ancaster stood as godmother to his first child.

Cleone Ancaster herself had 12 children, eight of whom were boys and four girls.

Contrary, no doubt, to general expectation, the long married life of David and Cleone Ancaster appears to have been extremely happy and prosperous.